PUFFIN BOOKS

The author of *World Cup WAGs* loves shopping, travel, fashion magazines and Italian designers, and she believes in fringed bikinis and floaty cover-ups. She lives in the UK with her husband and kids.

Also Available:

WAGs' World: Playing the Game
WAGs' World: Knowing the Score

World Cup WAGS

By Anonymous

PUFFIN

PUFFIN BOOKS

Published by the Penguin Group
Penguin Books Ltd, 80 Strand, London WC2R ORL, England
Penguin Group (USA) Inc., 375 Hudson Street, New York, New York 10014, USA
Penguin Group (Canada), 90 Eglinton Avenue East, Suite 700, Toronto, Ontario, Canada M4P 2Y3
(a division of Pearson Penguin Canada Inc.)
Penguin Ireland, 25 St Stephen's Green, Dublin 2, Ireland (a division of Penguin Books Ltd)
Penguin Group (Australia), 250 Camberwell Road, Camberwell, Victoria 3124, Australia
(a division of Pearson Australia Group Pty Ltd)
Penguin Books India Pvt Ltd, 11 Community Centre, Panchsheel Park, New Delhi – 110 017, India
Penguin Group (NZ), 67 Apollo Drive, Rosedale, North Shore 0632, New Zealand
(a division of Pearson New Zealand Ltd)
Penguin Books (South Africa) (Pty) Ltd, 24 Sturdee Avenue, Rosebank,
Johannesburg 2196, South Africa

Penguin Books Ltd, Registered Offices: 80 Strand, London WC2R ORL, England

puffinbooks.com

First published 2010
1

The moral right of the author has been asserted
All rights reserved

Set in Sabon MT 10.5/15.5 pt
Typeset by Palimpsest Book Production Limited, Grangemouth, Stirlingshire
Made and printed in England by Clays Ltd, St Ives plc

British Library Cataloguing in Publication Data
A CIP catalogue record for this book is available from the British Library

ISBN: 978-0-141-32996-3

www.greenpenguin.co.uk

To all the beach-lovers in my life. Keep on swimming.

1

Sun, sea and celebs. Amy Thornton was surrounded by them and she was loving every minute of it.

She took a sip of her blush-coloured fruity cocktail and scanned the impressive designer outfits the guests were modelling as they stood chatting and laughing in small groups. She knew she probably stood out a bit in comparison to them. Amy's micro-swimwear and maxi-sunglasses were more high street than high fashion, her hair wasn't professionally styled and her skin was almost translucent from a month of being cooped up at school taking exams.

But she didn't care. A beach party in a luxury resort on the Spanish coast was exactly what she needed right now.

She could do without the camera crew that was heading towards her, though. And the pushy reporter woman who suddenly invaded her personal space, firing questions at her with a wide, fake smile.

Amy took a few steps back from the grinning journalist and hoped she was still far enough away from the resort's huge infinity pool not to land with a splash. Not that it would be that much of a problem – she was a trained lifeguard, after all, for her Saturday job back home. In fact, maybe a sudden refreshing swim would be preferable to answering all these questions.

Amy tried nodding a lot in response, but the reporter clearly wasn't going to let her get away with that.

'So, Amy, how does it feel to be in the World Cup host country while your footballer boyfriend is relegated to watching the action from England?'

Amy gulped. 'Er, well, I'm only here for the first couple of weeks of the actual matches . . .' She wasn't sure what else to say. Especially since Damien was likely to watch whatever programme this interview ended up on. He watched anything and everything remotely World Cup related. He always had done, but now that some of his team-mates and friends were on the England squad, he was even more glued to the pre-tournament coverage than he had been four years ago, if that was possible. Amy remembered the football-mad boy-next-door that she'd secretly had a bit of a crush on even then, when she was only thirteen and he was fifteen. She used to think of excuses to talk to him, and asking who he thought would win the World Cup had been a good one.

In the distance, Amy saw her twin best friends Asha and Susila coming out of the clubhouse holding fresh drinks, including an extra one for her. She wondered about excusing herself to the journalist, saying she had to help her friends.

But before she could move, a stout man blustered in front of them, forcing the reporter out of the way.

Amy was about to smile in gratitude when the man boomed, 'Grant Maguire, *Sports on Saturday*. You're Amy Thornton, right?'

Oh no – more press. An even pushier team, by the looks of things. She knew there would be press at this party – it was the whole point, really, as the event had been organized by a television production company. But she really didn't expect them to be all that interested in her, not when she was sure there were *proper* stars around here. She and the twins had seen some major celebrities when they'd first arrived, though oddly there was no sign of them now.

The *Sports on Saturday* cameras closed in on Amy, blocking out much of the bright Spanish sunlight.

'Amy Thornton?' the man repeated. 'WAG to Damien Taylor, the Premiership's top midfielder, boy wonder at Royal Boroughs FC? That's right, isn't it?'

'Oh, yeah, Damien's a brilliant footballer,' Amy said, deciding to make the best of this if she could. 'And also, yes, I'm his girlfriend.' She didn't exactly relate to the term 'WAG' – it seemed to imply a lifestyle she couldn't afford any more, and actually never could. A fact that hadn't stopped her running up an enormous debt on her father's credit card last summer in a desperate attempt to keep up with the other 'wives and girlfriends' in London.

Asha appeared at Amy's side, her hands free of drinks now. 'Actually, Amy isn't just Damien Taylor's other half. She's a celebrity in her own right,' she declared with a flick of her dark wavy hair. 'And I'm Asha, Amy's best friend from Stanleydale. I'm young, free and single –' she winked into the camera – 'and I'm also a star on the bestselling *Absolutely Amy: Super-Fit!* DVD. As I'm sure you know. And if you don't, it's available in all good shops, well in the UK at least, and –'

The reporter ignored her. 'So, Amy! Why are you here in

the World Cup host nation without your footballer boyfriend?'

Amy sighed. Not this again. 'He . . . I . . .'

'Amy and I are here to film the next in our fitness DVD series,' Asha cut in. 'The *Absolutely Amy: Beach Fit!* team are shooting during the group matches and adding various DVD extras to tie in with the World Cup vibe. And most of the filming will be right near the England team's base.' Asha put her thumbs up and spoke straight to camera like a TV-presenting professional. 'Go, lads! The *Absolutely Amy* team is right behind you! Even if we're leaving after the group matches, you lot had better not!'

'Excuse me, I was interviewing Amy,' the reporter said to Asha.

'Excuse me, I was plugging our DVDs!' Asha smiled playfully. 'Don't you want to know more about *Absolutely Amy*?'

'I'm covering the World Cup,' the reporter said.

'Yeah, but it's related. Weren't you listening? Also our personal trainer is Josh Hunt, who used to work for the Royal Boroughs, which of course is England captain Danny Harris's team. So, about Josh . . . No, actually, you've probably heard all the rumours. I won't say any more.'

'Asha!' Amy hissed.

Asha gave her an innocent look and continued. 'The other stars are more interesting anyway. There's my twin sister, Susila, who does the beginner's moves to the right of Amy. She's great – very steady and sensible! And I'm Asha, the one who does the high-intensity workout on the left.' She laughed, brimming with confidence. 'You could say I'm Absolutely Asha, Super-*mega*-fit!'

'OK, thank you. That's all very interesting, Tasha.'

'Asha,' she corrected him. 'It's Indian.'

'That's nice.' The reporter said, giving Asha a tight smile. He aimed his microphone pointedly at Amy. 'So, Amy Thornton, you're just seventeen years old, is that right?'

Amy was glad she could nod her answers again.

'And your boyfriend is only nineteen, but an extremely talented player. A lot of people think he should have been selected for the squad. How does he feel about having been overlooked by England manager, Joe Vulkan?'

'Uh . . . he's . . .'

'He's fine!' Asha answered for her. 'He's happy watching the action at home with his mum.' She smiled. 'Everyone loves the World Cup! I'm not even into football and I love it. Come on, Eng-er-land!'

Asha stepped away and did a little England-supporting dance and the cameras turned towards her. Then Asha suddenly doubled back, grabbed Amy's arm and pulled her away before anyone could react.

'My name's Asha! Remember that! See ya!' she called.

Amy looked at her. 'Asha, what are you –'

'Shh, come with me.'

She led Amy down a narrow, winding path and through some shrubbery into a clearing. It led on to the most gorgeous beach Amy had seen in her life. Pebbles in myriad shades of grey and white glistened in the sun and the people standing around seemed even more glamorous than the ones they'd just left behind.

'Ha! Lost 'em!' Asha laughed. 'Susi, you're a genius.'

'Yeah, well, took you long enough to get away from the

cameras,' Susi complained from where she was waiting for her sister, balancing three drinks in her hands. 'Anyway, I told you there was an exclusive area. I've been watching the A-list disappearing through that gap in the hedge for the past half hour.' She looked at the drinks in her hand. 'I've spilt quite a bit, though, sorry. The ground's a bit uneven here.'

'Don't worry,' Amy smiled at her friend.

'Yeah, don't worry, we'll send you back for more,' Asha said. 'Bet *you* couldn't give that lot the slip like I can.' She mimed the reporters thrusting the microphone in Amy's face. 'They're a bunch of vultures. At least I managed to get in a huge plug for our DVDs. Should shift a few copies!'

'Asha, you're terrible!' Amy laughed. 'But thanks.' Amy was still giving all her share of the money from DVD sales to her dad. She needed every penny she could get to pay him back for the huge bills she'd run up on his credit card, plus extra for guilt. Especially because her dad didn't approve of Amy doing the DVDs in the first place. He was worried that it wasn't 'honest' work, not like Amy's lifeguarding at the local water park, but Amy's mother had talked him round. 'She's a hard-working lass,' Amy's mum had said. 'And she'll study hard the rest of the time. Give her a break. Besides, she can show young girls all over Britain that you don't have to be a size zero to be fit and attractive!'

'I'm the total DVD-plugging champion,' Asha crowed.

'Did you mention me?' Susi asked nervously. Out of the three of them, she was the least comfortable with the lime-light, and she'd only really gone along with the whole DVD thing because of her sister and her friend.

'Course I did,' Asha said. 'Don't look so worried – I said

you were great! And steady and sensible.' She grinned. 'I didn't say anything good about Josh, though.'

Susi gave her a stern look. 'Asha, he's our colleague – our trainer. Without Josh there wouldn't *be* an *Absolutely Amy.*'

'Course there would. They could have found a different, less annoying trainer. Fitter too –'

'Come on, you know he's gorgeous,' Susi said.

'Yeah, and big-headed with it. I can't believe it doesn't put girls off. And don't forget how he caused trouble for our Amy. I'm so glad I dumped him!'

'Ash, honestly, all that Josh stuff was ages ago. Can't you leave him alone now?'

Amy sighed to herself – she agreed with Susi. She really didn't want Asha to dredge up what had happened with Josh last summer, when he'd possibly tried to split up her and Damien, even dating Asha as a way to get closer to Amy. But no one knew for sure whether Josh was really guilty of those crimes, and she'd had enough of thinking about it, even if the gossip columns – and Asha – seemed determined to keep the rumours alive.

Tuning out Susi and Asha's bickering, Amy sipped her drink and stared at the gently lapping waves. This beach really was idyllic.

Until the sky darkened and the peace was interrupted by the unmistakeable din of a helicopter overhead.

'Paparazzi,' Amy groaned to her friends. 'God, I'd forgotten what this can be like. I've been right sheltered up in Stanleydale, especially since I was grounded half the time.'

'Yeah, but what about that time we went to London for the shoot?' Susi remembered with a shudder. 'They were chasing you down the street.' She put on a silly voice. '*Amy Thornton, where did you get your bag? Amy Thornton, Balenciaga or D&G?*'

Asha looked around. 'Relax, you two, they're not here for Amy. We followed the A-list, didn't we?' She nudged her sister and pointed somewhere behind Amy's back. 'See that lad over there? The tall dark one?' She gave a smug smile. 'It's only Rafael Badillo.'

'*The* Rafael Badillo?' Susi gasped. 'It can't be him, Ash. Surely he lives in Hollywood?'

'Yeah, but that lot get on planes the way we catch buses, don't they?' Asha shrugged. 'Only without the three-hour wait in the rain. Anyway, he's originally from a Spanish town called San Sebastian and he's got this "childhood-sweetheart fiancée" called Rena. I saw it in *Just Gossip*. It's him, honestly, I'd recognize him anywhere. Though the girl he's with right now doesn't look like Rena.'

Amy turned her head and sure enough, there was a very familiar and fit-looking young guy ignoring the commotion overhead as he kept his arm round a leggy blonde girl dressed in a peach-coloured Narciso Rodriguez stretch halter-neck dress that showed off her fabulous tan.

Then the girl moved, throwing her head back in laughter. And actually, she was extremely familiar too.

'Hey, hold on! Isn't that Rosay?' Susi asked at exactly the same time that Amy recognized her unlikely friend from last summer.

'It is!' Amy agreed. 'It's Rosay!' Rosay ('*like the wine*')

Sands was the step-daughter of Damien's boss, the Boroughs manager. She'd also famously broken the heart of ex-Boroughs top striker Scott White, who'd now transferred away from the UK leagues altogether. Amy and Rosay hadn't seen each other for ages, but they sent each other occasional texts. And none of the messages had mentioned dating an Oscar-nominated nineteen-year-old actor. An *engaged* Oscar-nominated nineteen-year-old actor.

Still, Amy knew Rosay well enough not to be particularly surprised. Her friend was now a famous singer after winning a reality show the year before. She was also pretty good at steering herself into the limelight with a string of celebrity boyfriends, none of whom ever lasted long. Her father was a renowned photography agent and Amy was sure he was partly responsible for all the coverage of Rosay and her conquests – and probably also for today's paparazzi. Usually Rosay denied any romance within days of the photos appearing, but it was a sure way to maintain a high level of media attention.

'Hey! Rosay!' Amy called.

But the helicopters overhead were multiplying and buzzing like genetically mutated flies, and Rosay didn't seem to hear her old friend across the beach.

'I can't believe she's here,' Amy said to Susi and Asha, raising her voice to make herself heard above the cacophony. 'Still, I suppose it puts me in my place a bit. No reporter's going to want to talk to me now, not when there's a scandalous relationship between a pop star and a movie star going on over there. 'Specially if it's Raf-Bad himself. God, half of our school has a crush on Rafael Badillo. Half of *England* has a crush on him.'

'Er, Amy . . .'

'What, Susi? It's true.'

'Yeah, OK, but half of England has a crush on *your* boyfriend too. And I think the press are heading straight for us again. I mean, for *you*, of course.'

Susi was right. There was a mass of people heaving camera equipment unsteadily across the shingle in their direction. Amy recognized the pushy man from before, together with his crew.

'Well, they won't be interested in me as soon as they see the scoop's over there.' Amy nodded towards the helicopters.

But the swarm of press stopped right beside her and gathered around.

The reporter pushed his way to the front of the group. 'Grant Maguire, *Sports on Saturday*,' he yelled. 'What do you think of the breaking news?'

'What, you mean about *them*?' Amy asked, tilting her head in the direction of Rosay and Rafael and wondering why they were asking *her* when she hadn't even seen Rosay for months.

Grant Maguire squinted into the distance, then straightened as the helicopters started to leave and the air on the beach gradually stilled.

'Hollywood gossip?' he boomed in the fresh silence. 'I'm from *Sports on Saturday*, not the Movie News Channel. No, I mean the latest about Ryan Clarke.'

'Ryan Clarke?' Amy frowned. 'The Wirral United winger who plays for England?' Damien always said he admired Clarke's ability, even though they were rivals of sorts.

'The Wirral United player who was seriously injured in

training,' Grant Maguire said, turning to the camera to continue his speech. 'The England player who Joe Vulkan has just pronounced unfit for play in this year's World Cup tournament. And with forty-eight hours until the official FIFA cut-off, Vulkan has just declared a replacement player.' He turned back to Amy. 'So how do you feel about that?'

'Oh, that's terrible for him,' Amy said, biting her lip. She knew an injury like that was Damien's worst nightmare. 'And all of Ryan Clarke's family and friends. They must be so worried.'

'That's very nice of you, Amy Thornton,' he said with an insincere smile. 'But *Sports on Saturday* would like your reaction to the last-minute addition to the England team.'

'Oh?' said Amy.

A slow smile spread on the reporter's face. 'Wait, hasn't he contacted you?'

When he said that, Amy automatically reached for her Donna Karan shoulder bag, one of Rosay's cast-offs from last year. Sure enough, her phone was glowing as if it had recently been ringing. She obviously hadn't been able to hear it over the roar of the helicopters.

The enormity of what the reporter was implying still didn't hit her until he turned to his team and called, 'This could be a good one!' He composed his face and began a glossy speech.

'Grant Maguire for *Sports on Saturday*, reporting on Playa Menor of the exclusive Las Playas resort at the moment in which seventeen-year-old Amy Thornton of Stanleydale, West Yorkshire, fresh from her school exams and partying with her young friends, hears that her boyfriend, Damien Taylor, has been selected for the England team.'

A dozen cameras and a sea of eyes turned to her as the reporter asked, 'Amy, how does it feel to find out that the hopes and dreams of our entire nation lie partly at the feet of your boyfriend?'

2

Amy stood outside the arrivals gate at Barcelona airport and pulled her baseball cap so low over her head that the peak nearly touched her oversized shades. She shrugged herself into the white cotton trench coat she'd bought in Topshop, an imitation of a Richard Nicoll one she'd seen on a television fashion show, and tried to look as invisible as possible.

It was brilliant that she'd be seeing Damien again so soon, and in such amazing circumstances. She'd been trying for weeks not to sound too enthusiastic whenever she spoke to him about her trip to Spain. The first reporter yesterday had the right idea – it felt plain weird to be jetting off to the World Cup's host country when her footballer boyfriend was stuck at home.

Not that Damien had expected to be picked for the England team, even though Amy thought he should have been, and told him so. He kept reminding her that he only had one cap to his name, earned for playing in the second half of an international friendly a few months ago, and he was a relatively inexperienced player after only one year in the Premiership.

But Amy thought he was being too modest. Maybe he wasn't quite Danny Harris, Royal Boroughs striker and team captain, who had recently also been appointed England captain. But the only other of Damien's team-mates to make Joe Vulkan's team was Steve Clifford, who was unlikely to get played unless something happened to England's number-one keeper, Alex Hills. Amy thought Damien was a miles better team player than Steve the goalie. Damien probably thought so too, but he hadn't seemed remotely miffed about it. All he'd said was, 'Good for Steve and Danny. They deserve it. I'm going to love watching football come home!'

'Yeah, but why don't you come with me to Spain?' Amy suggested then, for about the tenth time. 'I know I'll only be there while the group matches are on, but you could probably get into any match you wanted. And aren't you always telling me that you can't beat live football?'

'You can't,' Damien grinned. 'But, nah, I'm all right here, thanks. You'll be too busy filming to see me, anyway. And I've got my brand-new flat-screen, the one your dad told me is a right extravagance.'

'Your mum said it too!'

'I know, and she said it louder. Though it hasn't stopped her coming over to watch it.' He laughed and gave Amy a quick, gorgeous kiss before shrugging and adding, 'You know, if Vulkan had wanted me there, he'd have picked me for the squad, wouldn't he?'

And now he had. Amy wanted to jump for joy, but without drawing any attention to herself. When she'd finally spoken to Damien last night, she'd never heard him sound so nervous and excited. In fact, she'd had to spend half the conversation reassuring him that the whole thing wasn't a weird dream or an embarrassing mistake.

A thick stream of tourists poured through the automatic doors and then, on his own behind a large group, there he was. Damien, sauntering towards her, a sports bag slung around his tall, muscular frame and a holdall in his hand, his warm brown eyes picking out Amy in the crowd and lighting up in a huge smile.

'Damien!' she called excitedly, seconds before she remembered she wanted to keep a low profile. Oh, it was just too difficult.

He stopped in front of her, threw down his luggage and scooped her into his arms, accidentally knocking her hat off in the process. Her blonde hair cascaded down her shoulders as he kissed her passionately and she responded, not caring any more about who was watching and whether they'd be recognized.

It was so fantastic to be with Damien again. It had been a tough year for Amy, and she'd been more or less grounded for most of it, but at least she'd still been able to see her boyfriend from time to time. Her dad had a soft spot for the boy who'd grown up next door, and that was even before Damien had signed with a Premiership team and become a source of insider knowledge about players, managers and team tactics. Now Damien had his own flat in London, but he stopped in to see Amy whenever he was headed north for a match, or on rare days off. Amy often had to wrestle him away from her dad's drawn-out discussions about formations and league tables. It was easier to get Damien to herself on the occasional weekends she travelled south to record or promote her DVDs.

And now they'd have all summer together and it was amazing. Well, apart from the shoots Amy had to attend and the extremely important matches Damien would be playing. But Amy didn't want to think about that yet. The main thing was that Damien was here, in the same country as her. She kissed him some more.

A round of applause broke out, complete with cheering.

They separated and Damien looked bewildered. 'Oh. I think we've got an audience, Ames.'

He nudged his head towards the crowd that had gathered around them, forming a circle as if Amy and Damien were street performers. Most of the people looked like holiday-makers, and many of them were clearly trying to work out what exactly all the fuss was about. But the ones who'd cheered and clapped were wearing England colours and calling things like, 'Oi, Taylor, save your energy for the matches!'

And some of the others were definitely reporters.

Then the rapid-fire questions started, bombarding Amy and Damien like a series of punches.

'Damien Taylor! How do you feel about the *Absolutely Amy* DVDs? Are the rumours true that you had a serious fight with Amy's personal trainer last year?'

'Amy, why did you arrive in Spain with Josh and not with Damien?'

'Damien, what do you think of the way *Just Gossip* magazine dubbed your Amy's first DVD *"Super-Flirt"* because of Josh Hunt?'

Amy felt herself losing it. She took a deep breath. 'You know, Damien's been called up to play for England!' she told the nearest reporter. 'Why don't you ask him about that?'

'But I write for *Quick Treat*!' the woman answered. 'This is what our readers are interested in. And, actually, if you could tell us your favourite beauty products –'

'Amy.' Damien held her hand tightly. 'Come on. Let's just go.'

Amy let him lead her towards the exit where, as Damien had explained on the phone last night, a car was waiting to take him to Villa Dorada, the England team base for the first round of the World Cup. The car had been arranged by Joe Vulkan's staff and strictly speaking it wasn't there for Amy at all – she had turned up at the airport under her own steam. The England manager had recently made a statement declaring that wives and girlfriends wouldn't be welcome at the complex except on a limited number of days he himself specified. But Amy and Damien had talked about it last night and decided things might be slightly different for Damien, seeing as he'd only just arrived. Surely it wouldn't hurt for Amy to see him to the gates of Villa Dorada? And anyway, she was staying within walking distance, in the more modest but still lovely Hotel Madrid, so it made sense for them to travel together.

The driver gave Amy a look as he held the door open, but he didn't say anything, and soon the car was cruising smoothly through the dusty outskirts of a sun-soaked Barcelona.

Damien had his arm round Amy and was staring out of the window in silence.

Amy bit her lip, thinking about the reporters at the airport.

'I'm really sorry about all those questions,' she began. She felt partly responsible – after all, it was true that she'd arrived in Spain with Josh Hunt. Though she'd also arrived with Susi, Asha and a medium-sized production team, but the press didn't seem to care about that.

Damien turned towards her as the car stopped at a red light. 'Don't worry about it, Ames, really. We've been through this. We both know what it's like by now, with that lot.' He gestured to the window as if there were paps there. Come to think of it, there probably were – it wouldn't be the first time Amy and Damien had been photographed at traffic lights.

'I know, but they were horrible,' Amy complained. 'They ruined your arrival.' She took a deep breath. 'God, Day, you're here to play for England! I can't believe they didn't ask about that. You'll be playing football in front of the whole world!'

He smiled and pulled her tightly towards him. 'Shh, I'm nervous enough as it is.'

'So?' Amy said. 'It won't make any difference. Or it'll make you even better.' She knew what he was like – if anyone could focus in nerve-wracking situations, Damien could. He'd played his socks off in front of the scouts in Stanleydale in the matches that led to him being signed to the Premiership in the first place, while many of his team-mates caved under the pressure. Amy had skipped school to watch it, and it had been thrilling. There was no one on the pitch more self-assured than her boyfriend.

'Anyway,' Damien said. 'The press might have been full of

questions about . . .' He grimaced, but only a tiny bit. 'Josh. But they asked that stuff just seconds after taking a billion photos of us, you know . . .' He gave Amy a long kiss. 'So I don't really think they're in any doubt about the answers.' His voice was low as he ran a hand through her hair. 'Do you?'

She kissed him in reply, holding him close, and another thrill ran through her – he was really here! And he was gorgeous, and he was hers. She was the luckiest girl in the world.

The rest of the journey went by in a blink, and soon the car drew up outside the large gilded gates of Villa Dorada. When the driver opened the door and Amy and Damien climbed out of the car, two men in golfing outfits stepped forward. One of them was unmistakeably Joe Vulkan, England manager, his greying hair looking out of place with his youthfully trim, former-footballer physique. He was even more striking in person than he was on television, and Amy felt captured by his commanding presence. She guessed that the other man, a balding, shorter and distinctly less charismatic figure, was probably assistant coach, Mike Ascott. A young boy stood in the background, effortlessly holding two sets of golf clubs. It looked like the men hadn't intended to meet Damien's car, but were just passing by in the middle of a game of golf.

'Damien Taylor, welcome,' said Joe Vulkan in his clipped accent, shaking Damien's hand firmly. 'We are pleased you could make it.'

Amy gave a tiny laugh at that. As if Damien would have passed up this opportunity in a million years. But the look that Vulkan gave her wiped away her sense of humour. It wasn't annoyance, or even disapproval. It was something else – as if he'd sized her up in two seconds and found her lacking. It was unnerving. She found herself adjusting her clothes and wanting to hide behind Damien.

Vulkan folded his arms and nodded. 'I will leave you in the capable hands of my assistant coach and I expect I will be seeing you soon enough.' He turned to Mike Ascott. 'Good game. Let's play again tomorrow after training.'

The England manager strode past a group of security guards and into the grounds of Villa Dorada, his caddy scurrying behind him. Amy knew Joe Vulkan had been dubbed 'The Volcano' because of his famous angry outbursts – she'd seen some of them for herself on televised international matches, as Vulkan ranted wildly on the sidelines of the pitch. She tried to console herself with the fact that if he minded her being here, they'd know about it.

She soon gave up on that idea when Ascott turned his back on Amy and said, 'OK, Taylor, rule number one. No girls.'

'But I'm . . .' Amy said, trailing off when she couldn't think how to finish that sentence. 'His girlfriend' didn't exactly seem like enough, but she didn't like the way the coach had said that, as if Damien might be seeing hundreds of different girls and she was just one of his casual hook-ups. She'd been going out with Damien for three years now!

Ascott didn't even glance back at her.

'No girls at all. Except on approved days off, and you'll be told when exactly those are. But let me tell you right now, today is *not* one of them. Rule two . . .'

Amy tried to catch Damien's eye as the coach continued to rattle off a list that made Villa Dorada sound more like an army camp than the luxury hotel resort she could see it was. But Damien kept his gaze firmly on Ascott, his expression grim, interspersed with occasional nodding.

'OK,' the coach said at last. 'You can say goodbye now. Then I'll show you to your room, and then the team captain wants to meet you.'

'Damien and Danny know each other already,' Amy found herself blurting. 'They play for the same team.' She herself considered Danny Harris a friend. She was almost tempted to add that, to kill the horrible feeling that she had absolutely no right to be here, but Ascott spoke before she could.

'That's all very well, but Harris still needs to formally welcome Taylor to the squad.' The coach coughed. 'OK, I'll wait inside the gates.'

Amy swallowed hard as Damien held her tentatively, glancing nervously back towards the coach. He whispered, 'Oh no, I'm in trouble already.'

'I don't think so, Day,' Amy said quietly. 'It's probably just the way he speaks to everyone.'

'Yeah, I hope you're right. So, Ames . . . See you on my days off, yeah?' The kiss he gave her was over too quickly.

'Yeah, course. See you.'

He turned and walked away, and she hesitated, feeling strangely tongue-tied. Then she called, 'Good luck!'

But he was already inside the gates, walking with Ascott towards the grand entrance of Villa Dorada, and he didn't show any signs of having heard her.

3

'Can you hear me out there?' Josh blared over the thumping beat in his unmistakeable New Zealand accent. 'All you people pumping it up in your living rooms – don't give up! Just four more – and push it! Go, go, go!'

Josh looked every bit the enthusiastic personal trainer as he jumped on the golden sand in front of Amy, his supremely toned arms punching the air. His muscles rippled and his *Absolutely Amy* vest was bursting with, well, pure fitness. Amy had to admit it: Josh was deeply attractive. Occasionally it was hard to concentrate on the routines because his body was kind of distracting. Amy guessed that, no matter what Asha said about Josh being replaceable, his looks hadn't hurt sales of their DVD.

She pulled her mind away from those thoughts and focused on mirroring Josh's exercises. To the left of her, Susi was half-heartedly speed-walking on the spot and to Amy's right, Asha was adding bounces, leg raises and mega-energy high-intensity spins to everything Josh did, effectively making him look like a bit of a lightweight, which Amy knew was entirely intentional.

'You can do it! Your body will thank you!'

'Josh's won't. He's creaking like an old door hinge,' Asha commented loudly to Amy.

The producer, Jessie, who was dressed entirely in black and clearly struggling in the Spanish heat, appeared at the side of the open-air set and called, 'OK, thanks, guys! Time for a break.' To her assistants she said, 'Too much glow – it needs to look more effortless when the cameras roll. Touch up the girls' make-up and we'll start the shoot in ten.'

'Make sure you hydrate!' Josh called out with a smile. Amy wondered whether he ever left his fitness trainer act behind these days. She used to talk to Josh a lot about everything, back when he was a trainee sports psychologist on Damien's team, but now their relationship was strictly professional. They rarely discussed anything that didn't involve triceps, biceps or abs.

So she was surprised when he sauntered over to her side of the makeshift dressing room, which was a canopied area at the back of the beach. The twins were ready and had gone to get fresh bottles of water, but Amy was still being fussed over by the *Absolutely Amy* make-up artist.

'Hey, Amy, you're looking fantastic,' Josh said casually, without a trace of the lingering stares he used to give her last summer. Then, to the girl who was fiddling with Amy's hair and face, he added, 'Great job!'

The make-up girl giggled and blushed, then she excused herself and left. Amy brushed off a feeling of mild annoyance. Did Josh think she needed professional help to look fantastic? Then she felt annoyed with herself for even thinking twice about how Josh thought she looked. Maybe not being allowed to see Damien was sending her boy-crazy already.

'Hi, Josh,' she said politely. 'Enjoying Spain so far?'

'Yeah, it's awesome, being here when the World Cup's on,' he replied. 'There's just such a buzz everywhere. Actually, that's what I wanted to ask you about. Will you be watching the opening ceremony with the twins?'

Amy nodded. She'd been looking forward to it for months, ever since her agent had issued the DVD filming schedule and told her it would be a 'World Cup tie-in DVD'. The recording for the DVD was only supposed to take about a week, but then the team wanted to shoot 'Amy in the world', visiting places like the hairdresser's and the nail salon. The whole thing was being filmed in and around Barcelona, where the England team were based, and their budget didn't allow them to fly to Madrid for the live ceremony, but she and the twins planned to watch it on one of the big screens in a city-centre plaza.

'Great. Well, it's just that there's a huge party for it at Big Carl's, and Rosay would love to see you there. I promised her I'd ask. And I was hoping that, you know, maybe all three of you could come. If you wanted to.'

Amy felt confused. 'Oh, yeah – I saw Rosay at a beach party the other day. Does Big Carl have a place near here?' She'd lived at Royal Boroughs manager Carlo di Rossi's house in London for a while, together with his wife Barbie and his step-daughter Rosay Sands. But none of them had ever mentioned a house in Spain.

Josh shrugged. 'Not normally, no. But he's hired a villa especially for the World Cup.'

'Oh, right.' It still didn't quite make sense. 'But why didn't Rosay invite me herself?' Amy wondered aloud. 'I don't think she saw me at the party, but she could have called.'

'I think she's lost her phone. But anyway, she's been crazy busy,' Josh said. 'So she asked me to ask you, since I see you every day right now.'

'Busy doing what? Standing on the beach with Rafael Badillo?' Amy blurted out. 'I mean, sorry, yes, I'm sure she's got lots to do.'

Josh laughed. 'Oh, yeah, I saw those pictures in the paper this morning! Well, it's probably all part of it. Rosay's singing at the opening ceremony, you know, and being seen with someone like that will raise her profile even more. She's gonna be huge.'

'Rosay's doing *what*?' She couldn't believe it. A couple of days ago Amy had been a relatively normal Stanleydale girl, retaking her GCSEs in the sixth form. True, she was going out with a Premiership footballer and starring in a fitness DVD, but she didn't get to see Damien all that often, and no one mentioned the DVD much at school.

And now here she was, living a life where her boyfriend was playing for England and her friend was singing at the World Cup opening ceremony. She laughed at the whole situation. 'Oh, wow, good for Rosay!'

Josh smiled. 'I know! She was a last-minute replacement for a bigger star, but don't tell her you know that.' Josh was the son of one of Carlo di Rossi's closest friends and he knew the whole di Rossi/Sands family pretty well. In fact, Rosay had once revealed to Amy that her step-dad had originally invited Josh to London partly as a way to get him and Rosay together. As if that was ever going to happen. Instead, Rosay had secretly fallen in love with the now ex-Boroughs striker Scott White, who she then cruelly dumped. And Josh had made a play for Amy, and then Asha, without much success. Asha thought he was a total creep.

'So will you come to the party? You and the twins?' Josh prompted Amy, jolting her away from her thoughts. 'Some of your other friends might be there, you know. Trina Santos is staying with Rosay right now, and so is Kylie Kemp, though she might be out with her footballer fiancé.'

'Oh, right. Well, OK. Why not? I'll check with Asha and Susi, but we'll probably be there.' It would be great to catch up with her friends from last summer. Something was still niggling at her, though, but she couldn't quite figure out what it was.

Josh gave a satisfied smile and left seconds before the twins came back with bottles of water.

'What did Action Man want?' Asha asked, using one of her tamer nicknames for the fitness trainer.

'He invited us to a party at Rosay's, for the opening ceremony,' Amy replied. 'Her step-dad's got a place nearby for World Cup month.'

Asha whistled. 'Bet it's luxurious. Count me in! Susi can stay at the hotel ringing our mother and reassuring her that I'm already asleep.'

'Asha!' Susi put her hands on her hips. 'I want to come to the party too. I haven't spoken to Rosay for ages, apart from anything else. I quite like her.'

'Yeah, me too,' Amy said. And then she realized what was bothering her. 'But she's singing at the opening ceremony in Madrid.'

'Wow, seriously?' said Susi. 'That's amazing.'

'Huh?' said Asha at the same time.

'I know.' Amy frowned. 'How can she be at the party if she's in a different city? But Josh said Rosay wanted to see me. It doesn't make sense.'

Asha gave her a knowing look. 'It makes perfect sense, Amy,' she said sternly. 'Josh is using Rosay as an excuse. He's only gone and asked you out. Again.' She sighed. 'What's Damien going to do about it this time?'

'What's it got to do with him?' Amy said, a sinking feeling growing in the pit of her stomach. 'I'll sort it out myself. Damien doesn't even need to know.' As if Damien didn't have more important things to think about than who had asked his girlfriend to a party.

'Yeah, good luck with that,' Asha said sarcastically. 'It worked out well before, didn't it? When you and Damien nearly broke up forever.'

Amy sighed. 'OK, so I'll tell Damien. He'll understand.'

'You mean he'll understand that the "love triangle" all the papers are on about is alive and kicking?'

'Asha, leave Amy alone,' Susi protested. 'Who cares why Josh invited us, anyway? There will be other people at the party. We can still have a good time, with or without Josh.'

Asha shrugged. 'If you say so.'

4

If Amy had been impressed with the di Rossi residence back in London, which boasted a swimming pool, a gym and a courtyard with a clock tower, she found the place Big Carl and Barbie had rented for World Cup season absolutely astounding. It made the England team's Villa Dorada look like a cheap B&B. It was set in a vast landscaped garden that included vineyards, orange trees and a series of ornate fountains. There was an outdoor swimming pool with hot tub. And the house itself was so big that Asha joked about needing to catch a bus, or possibly a private jet, to get from one side to the other. There was also an incredible amount of security – possibly more than there was at Villa Dorada. The uniformed men dotted around the grounds were restraining vicious-looking guard dogs.

Even though they were late, Asha exuded her usual confidence as she strode past the security and towards the doorman at the main entrance. Amy hung back with Susi, grateful to have a friend who seemed as nervous as she felt. The reason they'd taken so long to get ready was that they'd pooled clothes and spent ages coming up with three suitable outfits for the party. Amy thought the results were pretty good, but it didn't change the fact that most of the items they were wearing were from New Look and Primark. Asha insisted it didn't matter, but Amy remembered what the other girls could be like. Not to mention Barbie di Rossi, Rosay's mum, who had threatened to call the fashion police the first time she'd met Amy.

'Come on, Amy,' Susi said, linking arms with her friend.

One of the dog-handling bouncers misread Amy's nervousness and said in a thick accent, 'You must not worry, they will not bite you! At least, not tonight. Usually they are free to hunt the invaders. Take care!' His laugh only added to Amy's worries, and she practically tiptoed past him and his dog.

Inside there was no sign of Barbie, or any guests at all. The three girls stood on marble flooring in a whitewashed hallway as a waitress clicked towards them holding a tray of drinks.

'Where is everyone?' Asha asked, helping herself to a drink.

'Private screening room,' the waitress answered. 'Is to your left.'

The room was easily as big as Screen 2 at the Stanleydale Multiplex. As the weighted doors shut very gradually behind Amy and her friends, there was enough light to see Big Carl at the front of the room, pacing about as if he was at the sidelines of Stadium Gardens watching a particularly stressful home match. He was holding a phone and talking heatedly into it. Meanwhile on the screen a group of colourfully dressed flame-throwers were giving it their all.

Then the doors snapped shut and the room went dark, lit only by the on-screen action. As the cameras panned away from the flame-throwers and focused on the black night cityscape, Amy and her friends couldn't see a thing.

'Oh, this is stupid,' Asha mumbled. 'Let's just sit anywhere. Here will do.' She ducked into the nearest row and stumbled forwards.

'Ow!' came a quiet male voice. 'Argh! What was that?'

Susi held Amy's elbow and giggled. 'I think she's sat on one of the guests.'

'I'm drenched!' the voice said. 'Did you just spill a drink on me? Argh!'

'Yeah, I did. There's no need to be such a baby about it.' Asha's indignant stage whisper floated towards them.

'Well, you could apologize,' the man said. His accent was a mixture of Spanish and American, and Amy thought she'd heard it somewhere before.

'Fine. Sorry. OK?' Asha's tone said 'case closed'. 'Honestly. Footballers!'

Susi nudged Amy as the ceremony lit up the room again. 'It's him,' she whispered.

'I'm not a footballer,' the voice said. 'I'm an actor.'

The screen filled with an image of a glittery Rosay on a white stage.

It was bright enough for Amy to see Asha's jaw drop as she stared at . . . 'Oh my God, you're Rafael Badillo!'

Rafael Badillo nodded, eyes dancing. 'Yes, I am.'

'Well, so what?' Asha mumbled, sitting down hard next to the actor with a dazed look on her face. 'I'm not going to go on about how great I think you are.'

'OK. In fact, be quiet, because Rosay's about to sing,' said Rafael Badillo, but he was smiling.

Amy and Susi scooted into seats next to Asha just in time for Rosay's soaring ballad to float across the room. Rosay was wearing a skimpy Roberto Cavalli fringed tank dress in a charcoal colour that set off her blonde hair extensions. She looked – and sounded – every bit the superstar she was fast becoming.

Halfway through the act, Amy glanced at her friends and was vaguely shocked to notice that Rafael Badillo wasn't watching his girlfriend on the screen at all.

He was looking at Asha.

Afterwards, the party quickly got into full swing. Waiters circled the guests with delicious-looking canapés and colourful cocktails, and people gathered in circles talking loudly about how amazing the opening ceremony was and how thrilled they were to be in the thick of the World Cup action. Carlo di Rossi himself mingled among the crowds, and at one point Amy heard him blare, 'I'll get the best recording I can for Barbie! It was momentous!'

Amy smiled to herself about how proud Big Carl sounded of his step-daughter, and then she briefly wondered what could possibly have caused Rosay's mum to miss it. Unless Barbie hadn't missed it at all, but just wanted a recording. Maybe Barbie was with Rosay right now, in Madrid. Amy tried to shake off the uncomfortable feelings as she remembered Josh's lies about how Rosay wanted to see her here tonight. At least Josh hadn't approached her yet – he was at the other side of the room talking to a group of Big Carl's friends. But he kept glancing over at where Amy was standing with Asha and Susi, and Amy knew it was only a matter of time before he came over.

She practised in her head the things she could say to put him off. 'Listen, I think we should keep things professional.' No, too businesslike. 'Josh, you know I've got a boyfriend.' No, too childish.

She was going through some other options when Rafael Badillo strolled over.

'Look, please could you just leave me alone,' Amy said, and then covered her hand with her mouth. She really hadn't meant to say it out loud.

Everyone stared at her.

'I'm so glad my fan club turned out in full force tonight,' Rafael said.

'Oh, sorry. I didn't mean you,' Amy said.

Rafael grinned his amazing film star smile at her. 'Don't worry, I can take it. As long as you don't start throwing rotten tomatoes as well.' He touched the damp patch at the side of his Paul Smith shirt, obviously from where Asha had spilled her drink. 'You're Amy, aren't you? Rosay has talked about you and your footballer boyfriend a lot.'

'Has she?' Amy said. Beside her, Asha was really obviously checking him out. Amy knew Asha had the biggest crush in the world on Raf-Bad. She also knew that worshipping someone wouldn't stop Asha speaking her mind.

Sure enough, Asha asked, 'How long have you been seeing Rosay, then?'

Rafael laughed. 'Not you as well. My press officer has had calls from every paper in the world asking the same question.'

'Did you give them the same non-answers?' Asha plucked a drink from a passing tray.

Rafael ducked theatrically, tugging at his shirt. 'No, not another drink! Please! Mercy!'

Asha narrowed her eyes at him.

Rafael straightened. 'Anyway, I haven't been seeing her long.' He looked at his watch.

'Oh, is that how you keep track of the lengths of your relationships?' Asha asked. 'Or do you have somewhere more exciting you need to be?'

'Maybe,' Rafael said lightly. 'Want to come with me and I'll show you?'

Amy rolled her eyes at Susi, and Susi rolled her eyes right back.

This would normally be Asha's cue to say something like 'What did your last chat-up line die of?'

But instead she just stared at him until he said, 'Is that a "yes"?'

Asha seemed to recover. 'Are all film stars as slick as you? Hollywood must be a very slippery place.'

Rafael laughed. 'You know what? It is. Come on, come with me. Just for a while. I'm going somewhere absolutely public and I promise I won't bite.'

'Yeah, you just try it. You'll regret it,' Asha barked, but when Rafael shrugged, said goodbye to all of them and started to walk away, she followed him, making sarcastic comments all the way.

Amy and Susi stared after them for a second.

'Omigod, what just happened there?' Amy said. 'Did Asha go off with a film star? One who's Rosay's new boyfriend?' She shook her head in disbelief. 'Should we go after her?'

'If there's one thing I've learnt about my twin sister in the last seventeen years, it's that she can look after herself,' Susi laughed. 'So yeah, let's give her two minutes and then find her.' But then she stopped laughing, nudged Amy and whispered, 'Josh is on his way over.'

'Oh no,' Amy whispered back. She really didn't feel like talking to Josh at all. Suddenly all she wanted to do was escape, find somewhere private and call Damien.

'I have to go. Er, really sorry, Susi,' she mumbled. 'You'll be OK talking to Josh, won't you?'

Susi nodded and Amy walked off quickly, not glancing back so that she wouldn't feel guilty. She found a side door and wandered out into the grounds, taking her phone out of her bag. She and Damien had been texting a lot for the last few days and she never knew when it would be a good time to call, but it was worth a try. She dialled his number and headed towards the fountain area.

He answered at the third ring and sounded so happy to hear from her that she hugged the phone to her ear. There were sounds of laughter in the distance at the other end, and she tried to imagine Damien in Villa Dorada, surrounded by all the famous footballers of the England team.

'I'm really missing you,' she told Damien.

'I miss you loads too, Ames,' he replied. 'Even though this is amazing, but it's also crazy. Remember how you thought Big Carl was bad, the way he controlled what I ate and what I did in my spare time? Well, you should see this lot! They won't even let us watch footy on telly half the time. They make us go to bed at ten!' He laughed. 'Mum gave up on that kind of thing with me and Stephen years ago!'

'Oh, wow. So did you get to see the ceremony?'

'Yeah, we got time off for it. We're in the middle of a huge party right now. Even Harris is letting his hair down for a change.'

Amy perched on the edge of a stone fountain and watched the water cascade around her as Damien told her all about the team captain and how uptight he'd been behaving, even worse than when he'd first left his wife. Amy stifled a slight feeling of guilt, listening to that. She reminded herself that Claudette Harris had got what she deserved after trying to blackmail Amy last year, and that Danny divorcing Claudette didn't really have anything to do with Amy.

Then Damien told her absolutely everything he'd been up to, like how he was being trained as a penalty taker and how hard he was working to try to impress Joe Vulkan, and how much he hoped he'd be played in the first match. She filled him in on the details of her days too. She even told him about Josh asking her to the party, though she carefully added that Rosay wanted her to go. He seemed fine with it. Then she chatted about seeing Rafael Badillo with Rosay on the beach, and how the actor had just walked off with Asha.

'Ha, I'm glad I'm not there now. Can you imagine a fight between Asha and Rosay?' Damien laughed. 'It would take a whole football team to restrain them.'

'I know. Susi and I said we'd find her . . .' A loud rumble overhead distracted her. Amy didn't think it could be paps this time – it sounded more like a plane than a helicopter, for a start.

'What?' Damien said. 'I can't hear you!'

'I can't hear myself either,' Amy yelled as the sound got louder. 'I'll ring again later, OK! Love you.'

She hung up and stared at the sky where, sure enough, a plane was coming in to land. As the noise level increased even more, Amy realized it seemed to be landing in a field right by Big Carl's house, or maybe within the grounds themselves.

Curiosity made her head towards the field, which was further away than it seemed. She'd been walking for about ten minutes when she reached it and saw immediately that it was an airfield, complete with a short runway on which a private jet had just landed. A group of people stood nearby in a tidy queue, like a receiving line at a wedding reception.

As Amy got closer, she saw that two of the people were Rafael Badillo and Asha. Big Carl was also there, smiling expectantly. She walked over and had almost reached them when Rosay appeared in the doorway of the plane, looking drop-dead glamorous in a sparkling red Oscar de la Renta strapless dress she must have changed into after singing. There was no sign of Barbie. Instead, Rosay was followed down the steps by her friend Trina Santos, who was tossing her mane of multi-coloured hair over the shoulder left bare by her figure-hugging one-sleeved Ashish outfit, and waving regally as if *she* was the singing sensation who had just starred in the World Cup opening ceremony. It was typical of Trina to try to steal the limelight.

'Hey, Amy!' Trina called, coming straight over to her as Rosay stopped to give her step-dad a hug and have a quiet conversation with him.

'Oh, Amy's here?' Asha turned, and Rafael mirrored her, shifting really close to Asha in the process. Amy could have sworn Asha noticed it, too – there was something about her smile.

Amy felt like telling Asha to be careful. Not just because Rafael's girlfriend was here, but also because the actor really seemed like trouble.

But now everyone was looking at her, including Rafael, so she just said, 'Yeah. Hiya. Wow, so Rosay's back already?'

'Course she is,' Trina said. 'Madrid's only a few hundred miles down the road. So, Amy, how are you? How's Damien? I heard he's in the England team! Did he tell you about my new baller boyfriend? Nik Sika, plays for Ghana? Me and you are both World Cup WAGs!' She laughed, flicking back her hair. 'And our men are both in Group B, like Kylie's Johann. The three of us are total rivals!'

Amy smiled nervously.

Then Trina seemed to notice Asha and Rafael. 'Oh, hey, Amy's friend from home! You're a fast mover, Raf.' She raised her eyebrows meaningfully.

'What?' Rafael said. 'Oh, no, we just met.'

'Exactly,' said Trina.

'I mean, we're not together,' Rafael explained, sneaking a sideways glance at Asha.

'In your dreams!' Asha said, shifting away from him.

Rafael coughed. 'OK, well . . . I should go see Rosay,' he said, excusing himself.

Trina laughed after he left. 'I can't believe you said that, Asha! He's so hot. I wouldn't mind, you know . . .'

Amy tried to hide her shock – after all, this was typical

attention-seeking Trina. 'But you just said you were with Nik Sika! And Rafael Badillo's going out with Rosay!' They'd had enough problems in the past, when Damien's team-mate Scott White had dated his way through a whole group of friends, causing all kinds of heartbreak.

'Well, yeah, I love my Nik to pieces. But still – he's Rafael Badillo! And Rosay's not really with Raf. It's a publicity stunt.'

'Does *he* know that?' Amy asked.

Trina shrugged. 'I don't think he'd care much, honey. They've only had, like, two or three dates, all fully chaperoned by the paparazzi. I think he's using her to make the break from his fiancée, you know – someone for the press to blame so he doesn't get to be the bad guy. Anyway, Rosay's about to dump him. She told me on the plane.'

'Really?' said Asha brightly.

Amy eyed her friend suspiciously.

'Yeah. She's probably doing it right now.' They all looked over at Rosay and Rafael, who did seem to be having a serious conversation. Rafael didn't exactly look heartbroken, though. He was nodding a lot and glancing around like he couldn't wait to get away.

'I don't know what's wrong with that girl,' Trina continued. 'She can't stay with anyone for more than five minutes, even if they're good for her career. Huh, she so doesn't deserve that singing success – not like me and the Miss Exes. I can't believe we barely lasted a month and she's huge!' She sighed, obviously thinking about the failed girl band she'd been in. 'Anyway, at least Rosay's actually *met* Rafael Badillo. Sometimes she doesn't even know the guys, you know – she just gets her photo agent dad to alter pictures so it looks like she's linked to some consenting A-lister. They both lap up the publicity and then deny the whole thing. Honestly, I think the closest Rosay's had to a proper relationship in the past year was when she pretended to fall in love with Scott White!'

Amy bit her lip. She was probably the only person who knew that Rosay hadn't been pretending about her feelings for Scott when she'd taken part in Trina's scheme to break his heart. Even Scott himself didn't know, and he'd run away from England altogether now to play for some mid-table Spanish team and escape the British press.

'That was scandal *gold* we dredged up about Scott and Claudette last year!' Trina laughed. 'Shame it caused a divorce – but Claudette Harris had it coming! Her scheming ruined more than a year of my life, and Rosay's too!' Her face twisted. Trina really couldn't stand Claudette and she'd relished seeing her crumble at the end of last summer. 'Anyway, I so wouldn't mind her ex – he's even more gorgeous than Rafael Badillo, and he's the England captain, so a bit higher status than my Nik! Plus, ooh yes, imagine how much it would annoy Claudette! Is Danny Harris seeing anyone new?'

Amy couldn't hide her shock this time. Trina was unstoppable! 'I don't know. I haven't seen Danny for ages, and Damien didn't say. I don't think those lads talk about girls and stuff. They just play football.'

'Yeah, right, honey.' Trina gave a throaty laugh. 'That's what they want you to think.'

Just then the ultra-glam Rosay appeared at Trina's side.

'Flaming cheek! That's the last time I try to be nice to a guy when I dump him,' she complained. 'He pretended he wasn't remotely bothered, then he said *he'd* been about to dump *me*. As *if*!' Then she threw her arms round her old friend. 'Amy! Amy, at last! I've been dying to see you. Did Josh tell you I lost my phone? And I've been so mega-busy that I got him to ask you to the party for me. I figured I'd make it up to you when I saw you.'

'Really?' So Josh hadn't been lying to Amy after all? 'But we saw you on the beach the other day. With, you know.' Amy nudged her head over to where Rafael was wandering away. 'Your boyfriend.'

'My *ex*! And oh, no, I'm sorry I didn't see you!' Rosay looked Amy up and down. 'Though if I had, I'd probably have said the same as I'm going to say now.' She took a deep breath and screeched, 'Omigod, Amy, what has happened to your *clothes*? Seriously, I need to take you shopping as soon as possible.' She leant forwards and said really quietly, just to Amy. 'Got some stuff to tell you. Soon.'

Then she looked around and said loudly, 'Right, let's ditch this place. I can't party with my step-dad hanging around. I'm single again! Who's up for some serious Spanish clubbing?'

5

Rio Grande was pulsating with a techno beat and strobe lighting when Amy, Rosay and Trina arrived. Asha wasn't with them – she said she wanted to stay with Susi because they needed to phone their mum, who always expected a goodnight call. Amy was just thinking it wasn't like Asha to remember this – Susi usually reminded her – when she saw Asha wandering off in the direction Rafael Badillo had taken moments before. It really didn't look like she had phone calls to her mother on her mind after all.

Amy wasn't worried about Asha and Rafael, though. Susi was sure to have got rid of Josh by now and she'd find her sister and keep her out of trouble, the way Susi always did. Amy sent her sensible friend a quick text explaining where she'd be and told her not to wait up. Susi was bound to drag Asha quickly back to the hotel room the three girls shared and they'd call home from there.

Meanwhile Amy was at Rio Grande. It had been Trina's idea to come here – her new boyfriend Nik had told her it was amazing. And Amy thought he could be right. She'd certainly never seen a club like it. From the wide doorway she could make out a shimmering stream running through the middle of the dance floor. It was flanked by snaking tendrils of plant life that formed an arched fence, maybe designed to stop clubbers falling into the water. A rainbow-coloured bridge gave the whole place a magical feel. It also had the effect of splitting the clubbers into two groups. Amy and her friends, who still hadn't cleared the door staff, were close to the calmer side. The other half of the club seemed completely wild.

'At last I can relax!' Rosay said, dancing on the spot already. 'I've had such a bad day.'

Amy frowned. 'But you've just been singing live in front of the whole world. That's pretty good, isn't it?'

Trina was studying her phone.

'I know.' Rosay shrugged. 'But my personal life is a mess, and . . . Look, I'll tell you soon, I promise. Right now I just want to dance.'

Amy glanced at the uniformed man by the entrance and lowered her voice. 'Um, are you sure they'll let us in? I mean, you two are OK, but I'm not eighteen yet and –'

Trina looked up and interrupted her. 'You'll never guess what? He's here! Nik's actually here! I sent him a text to tell him where I was, and he said "Snap"!' She looked around desperately until she yelled, 'There! Over there! Nik! Nik, babe!' Trina waved at an ultra-tall, lean and gorgeous guy who was propping up the brightly lit bar past the bridge. He was surrounded by some other men and a few glamorously dressed girls.

'My boyfriend, Nik Sika, is waiting for us,' Trina said loudly to the doorman. 'You know. The World Cup player.'

'Oh, you are with the footballers?' The doorman gave Rosay a nod of recognition. 'Of course.' He gestured for them to go in. He didn't even seem to expect them to pay. Amy had got used to this kind of treatment in London's exclusive clubs, but she hadn't expected it in Barcelona.

Trina waved to Nik as they crossed the room. 'Wow, he's right to say "footballers"! There are tons of them over there! Half of Group B, I think.' She stopped on the bridge to get a better look. 'Shouldn't they be fighting each other instead of drinking together? It looks like they get on better off the pitch than they do on it.'

'They'll get tanked first and fight later,' Rosay remarked, 'if I know ballers.'

'Oh, I don't know. Group B aren't that bad. England, the Netherlands, Paraguay, Ghana,' Trina rattled off. 'Loads of them are mates from the English clubs anyway.'

It was true. Amy recognized quite a few faces from the matches Damien watched constantly. One of them was Damien's Premiership team-mate, the Dutch player Johaan Haag, with his fiancée Kylie draped prettily over his arm. Kylie looked slightly different from the way she did last summer, but Amy couldn't say exactly how. Amy and Kylie had only really kept in touch by text during the year, but she knew Damien spent lots of time at Johann and Kylie's house in London. She suddenly felt a bit jealous that Kylie was with here with Johann when Amy wasn't allowed to see Damien. But Johann played for the Netherlands, not England, and his team must have different rules.

Then she noticed something, and felt even worse.

Some of the boys were actually England players. Including Steve Clifford, the Royal Boroughs goalie, who was standing with his new girlfriend, Lauren Thompson, an ex

WAG-wannabe who'd finally fulfilled her dream by stealing someone else's boyfriend a couple of months ago. Amy heard that Courtney, Steve's ex, had been devastated.

But weren't the England lads supposed to be at a party at Villa Dorada, like Damien said? Amy wondered whether they were breaking the rules, and if so what would happen if they were caught.

Or maybe some of the lads had been allowed out after all. In which case, where was Damien, and why hadn't he told her? She was dying to see him!

'Aw, Danny Harris isn't here, though. Never mind. Come on, I'll introduce you to my Nik,' Trina said, reaching the end of the bridge.

'No, forget footballers, Amy! Come and dance instead.' Rosay gazed longingly at the dance floor.

Amy took out her phone, but there was no sign of a call or a message from Damien. She wasn't sure what to do. Should she go with Trina or just dance with Rosay?

Really all she really wanted to do was find somewhere quiet, ring Damien and ask him what was going on.

Lauren, Steve the goalie's plastic perma-tanned girlfriend, waved at Amy and looked like she was coming over to talk to her. That did it. Amy wouldn't have minded chatting to Kylie, but Lauren was just annoying. They'd never been friends and Lauren had even tried to blackmail Amy at one point, but she seemed to have forgotten all about it now that she'd got what she wanted: a Premiership boyfriend. Lauren was probably on her way over to brag about spending Steve's money on something extravagant, and Amy really didn't want to know.

Trina and Rosay looked at her expectantly.

'Are you coming?' Trina asked.

'No, she's dancing,' Rosay said.

'No, I think . . . Uh, sorry, Trina. And Rosay. But I'll join you in a minute, OK?'

'Suit yourself,' Rosay shrugged. 'I know some of those girls. I'll be over there.'

Rosay headed for a group of stunningly dressed Ghanaian women on the dance floor. Meanwhile Trina was squealing and hugging the super-tall, smiling Nik Sika, though she still kind of looked around her the whole time, as if she was looking for someone better.

It didn't take Amy long to find the door to what was clearly some kind of chill-out room, dotted with sofas and dimly lit. As she stepped in, the relative silence echoed in her ears. She took her phone out, ready to ring Damien.

'Amy!' a voice called from a pool table at the end of the room. 'Hey, Amy, is that you?'

Amy squinted. 'Danny?'

Sure enough, it was the England captain himself, looking striking in a slightly dishevelled suit from his own Armani range. Amy knew for sure now that the whole of the England team must have been allowed out. Danny would *never* break the rules.

He strode over and gave her a hug. 'Wow, it's great to see you!' He smelled of expensive aftershave, but not a whiff of alcohol. Amy knew that Danny Harris prided himself on being completely sensible and dedicated to his sport. There was a reason he'd become the youngest ever captain of England. He acted older than his years – everybody had always said so. That was why the British public wasn't surprised when he and Claudette got married in their teens. They were more shocked that Danny got divorced in his early twenties, though no one blamed him, not after they read about Claudette's scandalous past. Danny's heartbreak had been widely reported in the papers.

'Where's Damien?' Amy blurted out. Then she realized how rude it sounded and she added, 'I mean, hello, it's great to see you too. How are you?'

'Not so good,' Danny gave a wry smile and dropped on to the nearest sofa. 'I just lost a game of pool. I was actually thinking of going back to Villa Dorada, but now you're here, I might stay a bit.' He smiled and patted the space beside him as if he wanted her to sit there.

Amy glanced around. There were enough lies doing the rounds of the gossip mags already. No way did she want any rumours to start about her and the captain of the England team. But everyone in here seemed busy doing their own thing, and anyway most of them were probably as much in the limelight as Danny, and not very likely to take mobile-phone pictures or sell made-up stories. There was nothing to feel uncomfortable about.

Even when she sat down and Danny put his arm along the back of the sofa behind her, so that it was almost around her. It was all perfectly innocent. Amy told herself off. She was always worrying about that kind of thing nowadays, and it was annoying that it got in the way of normal life.

Danny smiled at her. 'So, about what you asked. The lads tried everything to tempt Damien, but he didn't want to come out,' he said. 'He went on about needing an early night.

46

He's taking it all very seriously, you know. Which is good, of course. Damien Taylor always gives one hundred and ten per cent and he's an asset to the team. Joe Vulkan made a great decision there.'

Amy relaxed even more. Danny sounded like he was being interviewed on a sports programme. She'd chat to him about football for a bit and then phone Damien, if Damien wasn't already asleep.

Danny kept talking for ages, all about how excited he was to be in Spain and England's chances for the World Cup and who their greatest rivals were. Amy nodded and smiled in all the right places. She'd always liked Danny. She'd talked to him a few times, mostly on nights out with Damien, and he'd always been friendly and funny, if a bit sad since his divorce.

'So how are things going for you?' Danny asked. 'Claudy used to talk about you and all the other girls non-stop. I used to tune most of it out, you know. No disrespect.' He gave a light laugh. 'But it's weird, you know . . . I sort of miss it now.'

Amy wasn't sure what to say to that. She decided to focus on his first question. 'Oh. Well, things for me are, er . . . good.'

Danny nodded, but he looked like he was miles away. After a short silence he blurted out, 'God, I miss her so much!' Then he added quickly, 'Oh, no. Sorry. It must be the heat in here – it's gone to my head. Just as well I never drink, isn't it? I'd be telling you all kinds of things no one wants to hear.' He gave a sad smile. 'Except the tabloids.'

Amy suddenly felt loads of sympathy for him. His life must have been a nightmare with all the divorce stuff, and he'd had to put a brave face on it in public and play the top-class football everyone expected of him.

'Oh, I'm sorry about . . . you know. Claudette and everything.'

'Thanks.' He brushed his hands on his trousers nervously. 'Anyway . . .'

'Oh, hey, Danny, it's OK. You can talk about it to me. Honestly.'

'Really?'

'Yeah, course.' He looked so awkward and unsure that she felt a sudden desperate need to reassure him. 'Look, you don't even have to talk now. Give me a call sometime, if you want.'

'No, it's OK. I . . .'

'No, do, honestly.' She handed him her phone. 'Send yourself a text and then you'll have my number, just in case.' It occurred to her, slightly too late, that he could possibly take this the wrong way, so she added, 'Damien always says great things about you. We were both really sad about what happened.'

He pressed some buttons on her phone and then handed it back. 'Well, thanks, Amy. You're a star.'

He gave her a quick hug that was so normal and friendly that it made Amy feel bad for even thinking about possible rumours, or Danny misinterpreting her offer.

'Want to go and dance?' he asked.

Amy couldn't hide her surprise. 'Why, do *you*?'

Danny laughed. 'Hey! I'm a sportsman – I could probably

win *Strictly Come Dancing* if I tried! Besides, I've got my glad rags on, haven't I? And our first match isn't until Wednesday. There's loads of time to recover from dance-related injuries. Come on.'

6

It was well past three in the morning when Danny's driver dropped Amy back at Hotel Madrid. She'd had a seriously great time dancing on the wild side of Rio Grande, mostly with Danny, but also with Rosay and a group of others. Trina and Nik had already gone by the time Danny and Amy left the chill-out room, and Rosay left too after a couple of hours, but Amy had just carried on enjoying herself until she admitted to Danny that she was exhausted and he offered to call his driver for her.

As they walked out together, Amy had a brief panic about paps and she made sure she stood as far from Danny as possible as lights flashed in her face. But then she felt annoyed about it. She had nothing to hide! Anyway, the press were so full of stories about her and Josh that they probably wouldn't think to link her to Danny Harris as well. It was all so ridiculous.

Now she was dying to kick off her high-heeled tie-front shoes, a sale bargain from a department store in Leeds. They pinched her feet in a way that the designer shoes she'd owned last year never had. She'd been so sad when she'd had to admit the Manolos were worn out and she wouldn't be able to buy any more, but she'd tried not to show it to her friends and family in Stanleydale. She knew she shouldn't have even bought the Manolos in the first place, using money she didn't have.

Amy hesitated at the door of the room she was sharing with Asha and Susi and wondered about calling Damien from the hotel corridor, so as not to wake the twins. Then she remembered how late it was – he'd be fast asleep. She sighed and slipped the keycard into the reader.

After stopping in the doorway to shed her shoes, she tiptoed around the dark room getting her things together as quietly as possible. It was only when she was halfway to the en suite with her make-up removal kit that it occurred to her. The room was quiet. *Too* quiet. She couldn't even hear breathing sounds. And from what Amy could see of the beds, they were too neat too. Susi would normally have kicked off her covers by now and Amy should have been tripping over them on her way past.

Snapping on the bathroom light confirmed Amy's suspicions. The other two beds were empty. The twins hadn't come back.

She put the main light on and sat on the edge of her bed. Were they OK? Should she call them? Or should she leave them to it? She didn't want it to seem like she was checking up on them. She wasn't their mother.

Then she remembered Asha walking off in search of Rafael Badillo, the newly single actor who was smoother than Amy's skin after the luxury facials she used to have at the spa.

That did it. She decided to try Susi first. Susi always knew what to do, and she'd reassure Amy in an instant. Maybe Susi had taken a long time to find Asha in those huge grounds, but they were probably on their way home right now.

The phone rang for ages and Amy was just starting to panic when Susi answered.

'Amy?' she asked breathlessly. 'Sorry, I was nowhere near my bag. Hey, why are you calling? Aren't you out clubbing with Danny Harris?'

'Oh, thank God you're OK!' Amy said. Then she realized what Susi had said. So much for rumours not starting, and in world-record breaking time too. 'Who told you about Danny?'

'Rosay and Trina and their mates. They came back from the club and started partying here instead. Rosay said she'd left you there with Danny.' Susi's voice was filled with surprise as she added, 'Hey, did you really think I might not be OK?'

'No, sorry, I knew you'd be fine. You always are! I'm so glad you're there to take care of Asha, too. So the party's still going?'

'Yeah. Full swing. Apparently this is totally normal for Spain. I don't exactly know when anyone *sleeps* around here.' She laughed. 'And I don't exactly care.'

Amy suddenly realized how light and bouncy her friend was sounding. Susi was normally so sensible and grounded. 'Susi, are you up to something?'

'What? No!' Susi giggled. 'I should ask *you* that, dancing with the England captain all night.'

'There were loads of other people around too. Anyway, don't change the subject. What are you up to?'

'Nothing. Just talking to Josh.'

52

'Oh, sorry I dumped him on you.' Amy felt a wave of guilt. 'What about Asha? Couldn't she help you lose Josh?'

'She was last seen disappearing into a darkened screening room with a certain famous actor,' Susi said casually.

'Omigod! Really? No way! You'd better rescue her, Susi! Bring her home. I'll put the travel kettle on for you both.'

'Amy, listen to yourself! They're showing some old football match and Big Carl is in there. Asha's fine. *I'm* fine. Get yourself some not-needed beauty sleep and we'll see you at the shoot in the morning.' She giggled again. 'I mean, in a few hours.'

There was silence.

Amy checked her phone. Susi had hung up on her. There was a text, though, which must have come through while she was talking to Susi.

It said: 'Thx. Danny x'. It was nice of him to send it, but she decided not to reply – she should probably leave it there. She wouldn't even bother saving Danny's number to her contacts. She'd better play it safe, just in case.

She thought about heading back to the party to see what her friends were really up to. Then she wondered about turning up at Villa Dorada instead. Maybe she could wake up Damien and surprise him.

But she was really tired and anyway, even if security at the villa let her in, there was no way Damien would be happy to see her. He'd just tell her this was his big chance and he needed to take it seriously, which meant no going out at all, even with his team-mates. Even if it meant that tomorrow's papers could be full of photos of her and Danny Harris on the dance floor together.

Being the girlfriend of an England player was proving to be a bit of a worrying let-down so far.

The next day started with three text message alerts, first on Amy's phone, then Asha's, then Susi's. It was like a Mexican wave of ultra-loud beeps that woke Amy up instantly, but didn't even make Susi or Asha stir.

Well, at least the twins were back. Amy had no idea when they'd got in. She could just see the outlines of their bodies in the single beds either side of her. They were out for the count.

Amy sat up and reached for her phone on the bedside table, knocking over half the contents of her bag in the process. The clattering still didn't cause any movement in her comatose friends.

The message was from Jessie, the producer of *Absolutely Amy: Beach Fit!* It said: 'Crew down with food poisoning after last night in the square. Day off! Shooting starts again tomorrow, usual time.'

Amy looked at the time. It was just as well today's shoot was cancelled – she'd totally overslept anyway. She stretched and wondered what she would do instead. Maybe explore Barcelona a bit; see the sights. Though probably not with Susi or Asha, who looked set to spend the day dreaming for England.

She decided to get ready and go to the hotel swimming pool, which was tiny and shaped like a mermaid. It looked lovely, but it wasn't very satisfying to swim in. After three short lengths, head-to-tail, Amy gave up and headed for the changing rooms.

When she'd dried and dressed, she stopped at the comfy chairs in the hotel lobby and decided to make some calls from there, where there was no chance of disturbing the sleeping twins. First she rang Damien, even though she knew he was unlikely to answer. He'd probably be in the middle of some serious training. It was worth a try, though.

Sure enough, it rang and rang until it went to voicemail. She left him a message telling him she missed him and how much she was looking forward to seeing him next time he had time off. She didn't mention that she knew he'd been allowed out last night. She supposed it was pretty admirable that Damien was so dedicated to his sport that he wouldn't even take one night off. It was Damien all over, really. Danny Harris was right – her boyfriend was an asset to the team.

Next, Amy called home. She had a long chat with her mum and dad about how everything was going, although her dad didn't really let her speak much. He mostly wanted to talk about the England squad and how he hoped Damien was taking his training seriously. Amy sighed as she agreed with her dad that this was really the most amazing opportunity in the world for Damien. By the time she hung up, she felt like having a good old non-football-related gossip with a friend instead.

She scrolled down her list of contacts. The number she had for Rosay was for the lost phone and she'd forgotten to ask Rosay for a new number. It was annoying because every single time Rosay had stopped dancing and spoken to Amy last night, she'd increased the air of mystery about whatever it was she wanted to tell her. She kept saying 'I'll explain later', and right now could have been the perfect time. Amy wondered about turning up at Big Carl and Barbie's villa unannounced, but she'd probably be eaten alive by the guard dogs before she could even explain who she was. Besides, Rosay had probably flown to some other city by now from her private airport.

But Kylie or Trina might be there. Of the two, Amy definitely preferred Kylie, who was slightly vacant, but at least wasn't constantly scheming against the other girls. She found the number and called it.

Kylie's voice was business-like when she answered. 'Kylie Kemp's phone. Who are you and how can I help you?' she chirped.

'Kylie, it's me, Amy. Don't you have caller display on your phone?'

'Oh, yeah, course I do. But Rosay said she'd lost your number when she lost her mobile, so I wasn't sure whether it was really you or some stranger who'd found her phone.'

'Huh?' Amy said. She'd forgotten how confusing Kylie could be. Kylie hadn't got her reputation as being a bit empty-headed for nothing. 'But it was Rosay who lost her phone, not me.'

'Yeah, I know *that*,' Kylie giggled. 'I'm not stupid! So is that really you then, Amy?'

'Er . . . yes.'

'Great! I haven't seen you for ages!'

'I was at Rio Grande last night. We had a ten-second chat before you and Johann showed me some salsa moves you'd just learnt. You told me you were all set to audition for *Strictly* next year, but you'd had to cancel it for some reason.'

56

'Oh, yeah, that's right. Sorry! I'm a bit dippy right now,' Kylie sighed.

Right now? Amy thought, but she didn't say it.

'I've got problems,' Kylie added sadly. 'Well, one big problem. Or one quite little problem.' She hesitated, then shouted, 'Poshie!'

'Oh, is it about Poshie?' Amy knew how attached Kylie was to her little pug. 'You must be really missing him.'

'Not really. He's right here. Which is part of the problem. Poshie! Get away from the antique thingie and come over here! Auntie Amy wants a word.'

Amy stifled a laugh as she heard clattering in the background, followed by doggie panting and slobbering noises.

Kylie came back on the line. 'Poshie said hi.'

'I heard,' Amy smiled. 'Tell him I said hi back. So what Poshie problems have you got? He sounded OK to me.'

'Oh, it's . . . a long story,' Kylie said.

'You as well?' Amy found herself saying. 'Rosay was being mysterious too! No one tells me anything.'

Kylie laughed. 'Well, I don't know exactly what's going on in Rosay's glam life, but I can definitely tell you some of my problems. In fact, you can help me out, starting right now! Fancy hitting the shops?'

'Yeah, sounds good,' Amy said.

'I can't take Poshie with us – he's been way too jumpy since we got here and I don't trust him in foreign streets! Hopefully he'll be OK here by himself for a bit. Poshie and I have a whole wing to ourselves, you know. Well, with Trina.'

'Wow. That's nice of Rosay's family.'

'Well, yeah, I think Big Carl put us miles away from the main house because our men don't play for England!'

'Oh, yeah. Course.'

'And it's nice here, but . . . when I'm not here and Trina's out, Poshie seems to get a bit freaked.' She lowered her voice. 'A couple of times I've found him in a state when I've got back.'

Poshie gave a yap as if he agreed.

'Oh no! Can't you stay somewhere else, then?'

'Not really,' said Kylie. 'The other Dutch families are in a hotel complex that doesn't allow dogs, and I think it would be hard to find somewhere else right now.' She sighed. 'Anyway, yeah, I need to visit some of the most exclusive boutiques in Europe! You'll love it.'

Amy agreed, made arrangements and hung up before she remembered she couldn't afford to go shopping at all, let alone in the kinds of places Kylie meant. She shrugged to herself and got ready. She wouldn't have to buy anything, after all – she was just helping out a friend who didn't want to shop alone.

7

Amy stood at the meeting place she'd arranged with Kylie, in a wide boulevard called Las Ramblas. It was flanked by coffee and pastry shops and boutiques housed in amazing-looking ornate buildings. There also seemed to be some kind of parade going on, and the pedestrianized area was filled with colourful floats displaying tall wooden figures all moving to the thumping beat of loud Spanish pop music.

She was admiring a skyscraper of a dragon on a passing street performer's head when a limo pulled up in the side street nearest to her and Kylie stepped out, immediately followed by Trina Santos and Lauren Thompson. Amy stifled a groan. Kylie hadn't mentioned she was inviting anyone else on this shopping trip.

Kylie looked the shining picture of health in a flowing flowery tunic teamed with leggings and thigh-high boots. Amy realized now what was different about her – she was definitely curvier than she'd been last summer. Maybe she'd had some plastic surgery. Amy knew Trina Santos and Lauren Thompson had both had boob jobs and were proud of it. They looked as glamorous as Kylie, only in far more figure-hugging outfits. In fact, Lauren was halfway out of her dress, but Amy decided not to mention it as it was probably intentional.

'Amy! Yay!' Kylie said, reaching over for an air-kiss. 'Hope you don't mind that I brought the others along. I need all the opinions I can get for this, even theirs. Oh, no offence, Trina and Lauren. You know I love you loads!'

Trina rolled her eyes, but Lauren said eagerly, 'Of course, Kylie! I'm so honoured you asked me along today. Though obviously I can see why you did, since I have fantastic fashion sense.' She smoothed out her clothes and stuck her nose in the air. 'You know, Stevie was telling me only the other night that he thought I could probably design my own line of clothes if I wanted to.'

It was Amy's turn to roll her eyes. Lauren was hard work. She always had been, but gaining the WAG status she'd craved for so long had made her a hundred times worse. Now she thought she knew *everything*.

'And I said to Stevie: you're right, it would be like a service to girls everywhere. I could help some of the sad wannabes who don't have much of a clue about style. You know, there's really no excuse – I used to be a poor personal assistant, but I still knew how to dress right. Even if it took a month's salary to buy a belt, you know, I knew if I bought quality key items it would be worth it . . .' She trailed off and looked Amy up and down, just as Rosay had done last night. Somehow, coming from Lauren, it was way more irritating. 'Actually, Amy, maybe I could give you a few tips.'

'I think the other way round is way more likely,' Trina laughed, tossing her multi-coloured mane. 'Look, are we going to stand here watching the parade go by or are we going to get Kylie to give us her own fashion parade over at the wedding boutique?'

'Yeah, let's go!' Lauren said, barely even noticing Trina's put-down. She'd always had a very thick skin. It had been useful for her when she'd been busy pursuing someone else's boyfriend. Courtney, Steve's ex, hadn't exactly given up without a fight, but Lauren had brushed off all the angry words and dagger-looks pretty easily.

Amy realized what exactly Trina had just said. 'Hold on!' she exclaimed. '*Wedding* boutique? You didn't tell me you were shopping for your wedding, Kylie.' She thought Kylie and Johann's wedding was all sorted now – she and Damien had already received an invitation on gilded satin-look paper. It was going to be a lavish do in a castle in Wales, and it had been arranged for the end of July in just a few weeks' time to coincide with Johann's extra-short off-season this year – and the availability of *Just Gossip* magazine, who'd bought the exclusive. They were set to feature the wedding and its 'Precious Gold' theme in their summer edition. Kylie had been texting Amy about it for months, telling her everything, including details of the 24-carat spun-gold tulle wedding dress that was being tailor-made for her by an up-and-coming young Italian designer.

Kylie led the girls down the uneven street, striding confidently in her low – for her – heels. She protested to Amy, 'No, I did tell you! I said we were going to some of the most exclusive boutiques in Europe. So that would be *wedding* boutiques.' Then she bit her lip and looked slightly guilty. 'Oh, wait, yeah, I don't think I told you that my wedding's been brought forward a little. And, er, moved to Spain. And I need a new dress.'

Amy was shocked. 'No, you didn't tell me that.'

'Oh. Well, I was about to. It's the day after the final. In case the Netherlands get that far. Though I'm sure they will.'

'Nik's team definitely will,' Trina remarked.

'I doubt it! But England will, won't they, Amy?' Lauren linked arms with Amy. 'England are the best! Well, Steve is, anyway. Damien's really a bit young and *inexperienced*, isn't he? But the rest of the team can carry him, I'm sure.'

Amy was too busy reeling from Kylie's revelation to react to that. 'But what about your gold dress, Kylie? And *Just Gossip*'s Summer Special and the castle in Wales?'

'Oh, never mind that! This is going to be a proper fairy-tale wedding! Well, although we have to do some legal stuff in a register office before, and maybe we'll renew our vows in Wales sometime as well,' Kylie said, as a photographer leapt out in front of the girls and started snapping. 'But anyway, we've found the perfect Spanish castle, and *Just Gossip* are pleased that it'll be so high profile right after the World Cup.' She smiled and posed for the camera. 'And we can still go on the exotic honeymoon, and everything else will be exactly the same, more or less. Except the dress. Which is why we're here today!'

'That gold tulle takes a very long time to shape, Amy,' Lauren said slowly, as if she was explaining something to a very small child.

Kylie sighed. 'No, it was almost ready, but it needed some alterations for my fuller figure and they didn't seem too happy about it, so . . . I decided I needed a whole new dress.

Oh, do you like my new-look boobs? Aren't they fab? I love them!' She laughed. 'Hey, and this way I get to go shopping with my friends! I just wish Paige was here. She should definitely make it out of the clinic in time for the wedding, though.'

Everyone made concerned noises about Kylie's best friend, ex-WAG Paige Young – even Trina who'd been Paige's absolute rival until Paige had collapsed with a serious eating disorder, one she was still recovering from. Then suddenly Trina had pretended to be a close and caring friend, especially when the press were around.

The photographer took a few more shots before he walked off, satisfied.

Kylie led the girls to a nearby boutique with an intricately styled ivory wedding dress in the window. She rang the bell and an assistant in a clingy black dress ushered them all in. They were shown straight to a plush dressing room where Trina and Lauren made themselves at home on high-backed chairs. Amy perched next to Trina, thinking about Kylie's news.

It was soon clear that the boutique had been expecting Kylie, as with only a few words of broken English another smartly dressed assistant appeared, holding a soft-looking white ball gown with a jewelled neckline. It was delicate and beautiful, but it wasn't tulle spun from 24-carat gold.

Amy frowned as the assistant gestured to the changing area behind the thick green curtain. 'I still don't really get it, Kylie. I thought you were set on that wedding. You've been planning it for nearly a year! What changed?'

Kylie sighed, fiddling with a tassel on the edge of the

curtain as the assistant stood patiently to one side. 'Well, see . . . I made a mistake.'

Lauren looked up from inspecting her nails and pretended to look sympathetic.

'She got the wrong sort of pet passport for Poshie,' Trina explained, managing to control her face so that only Amy noticed the twitch of laughter on her lips. 'He was allowed into Spain, but now he can't go back to Britain until he's had a different set of injections and waited six months. It's either that, or he has to go into quarantine at Heathrow. So . . . Poshie wouldn't be able to make it to the wedding in Wales.' Trina arranged her features into a sympathetic expression.

'Oh no!' Amy knew how bad that was. Kylie's pug was like a child to her. 'Are you going home without him?'

'I'm not sure yet.' Kylie looked like she was going to cry. 'But whatever happens, I definitely need Poshie at the wedding. Apart from anything else, he's a pageboy! I have his outfit ready and everything.'

'But couldn't you just postpone the wedding? I mean, have it after Poshie's back in Britain, in a few months' time?'

'No, no, it wouldn't work,' Kylie said firmly. 'It's got to be as soon as possible. Johann agrees. And the people at *Just Gossip* said, if we don't want to clash with other celebrity weddings, that date will be perfect.' She nodded at the assistant, took the dress and pulled the curtain closed behind her.

Trina shrugged at Lauren and Amy. 'Perfect for extra media attention,' she said quietly, sounding a tiny bit jealous.

Lauren sighed in even more obvious envy and didn't lower her voice as she said, 'Wow, yeah, can you imagine the kind of press coverage it's going to get right after the World Cup final? Kylie is so lucky!' She studied her reverse French manicured nails. 'Though I'm sure my Stevie would do the same for me in a heartbeat.'

Trina caught Amy's eye and gave a snort, which she quickly turned into a cough. Then Kylie drew back the curtain and the fashion parade of breathtakingly beautiful dresses began.

8

The *Absolutely Amy* crew's food poisoning turned out to be genuine and not just a result of too much partying for the opening ceremony. With half the staff still out of action, Jessie the producer was forced to cancel another day's filming. She swept around the beach area in a panic, ranting about running over schedule and probably needing to book everything for longer than the two weeks they'd originally planned.

Not that Amy would mind that at all. She'd already been wondering how she could stay in Spain as long as Damien did. Even though England's first game wasn't until the next day, Amy was already sure that they would get through to the final sixteen and further. Her original plans to rush home and watch the knockout rounds with Damien on his new telly had completely changed. Now she was planning to be at all the matches, live, to cheer Damien on. She just wasn't quite sure how she was going to pay for the hotel once the production team stopped covering her expenses.

The producer left in a flurry of black clothes and with instructions for everyone to be back tomorrow, crew or no crew. Josh said he needed a word and followed her towards the bar area.

Susi watched them walk away before she turned to her friends. 'What are we going to do today, then?'

Asha shrugged at Susi and gestured around her. 'Sand. Sun. Day off. I don't know, what do you reckon?' She pulled a sunlounger away from the neat row, unfurled her towel over it and snapped a pair of sunglasses on to her head.

'Yeah, good idea, Ash,' Amy said, settling on the sunlounger next to her.

Susi shrugged and sat the other side of Asha.

Amy took a large bottle of suncream out of her bag and started applying it. She was still much paler than anyone else she'd seen since her arrival in Spain and she did not want her skin to end up matching her bright red swimsuit.

She glanced at her friends. 'Hey, now I've got loads of time to get the full scoop about Rosay's party,' she said.

So far, Asha and Susi hadn't answered Amy's questions about it properly at all. They just kept saying they'd had a good time and got in really late. When Amy asked Asha specifically about Rafael, her friend just said, 'Oh, that smoothie thinks he's God's gift.' Weirdly enough, Susi didn't seem remotely interested in what might have gone on between Asha and Rafael, and without backup for her probing, Amy soon gave up.

But now she had all day to interrogate Asha, and would get the truth out of her somehow.

'So, Asha, come on. Tell me what really happened with you and that famous film star.'

'I'm busy. I'm relaxing,' Asha said, her expression unreadable behind her sunglasses. 'And why don't you tell me what really happened between you and that captain of the England team?'

'Asha! I told you me and Danny just danced. In a big group of people, mostly.'

'And I told you nothing happened with Mr Big Ego.' She turned towards her sister and said, so quietly that Amy nearly missed it, 'Yet.'

Amy expected Susi to jump on that and make a huge fuss, but Susi was perched on the end of her sunlounger staring at the sea and acting like she hadn't even heard.

Amy sighed and decided to do Susi's job. 'Asha, you know, Rafael Badillo looks like trouble.'

'So does Danny Harris,' Asha said. 'Especially when you're going out with someone else on his team. And his ex-wife has always had it in for you.' She lifted her sunglasses and nodded at Amy as if to say she'd won. But then she sighed. 'Rafael's out of my league, isn't he, Amy? I know you're thinking it.'

She sounded so sad that Amy found herself saying, 'No way! If anything, it's the other way round.'

'You think?'

'Course!' And then Amy found herself reassuring her friend about Rafael, even though she'd wanted to warn Asha away from him. This was going all wrong. Why wasn't Susi joining in and helping her?

'Listen, I'm going to the bar,' said Susi, standing up. 'Anyone want a drink or an ice cream or anything?'

They gave Susi their orders and then Amy lay back, adjusting the sun umbrella slightly to give herself some shade. She didn't care how pale she was – it would be a disaster if she got sunburn and ruined tomorrow's shoot. Plus she didn't want to be in pain for the first England game.

Asha seemed lost in thought, or possibly asleep, so Amy left her to it and concentrated on relaxing. A beach vendor approached her, carrying a wooden board laden with cheap-looking hair accessories and jewellery. He stopped right in front of her and rested the board in the sand, making it hard for Amy to resist looking through the colourful objects he was selling. After thinking about it for a while, she fished a couple of euros out of her purse and spent them on a string of red and white beads that she thought would look great with her newest favourite Primark top. The top was pure white and filmy, and if she wore the necklace with it, she'd be in England colours. It would be perfect for tomorrow's match.

After the man left, Asha laughed. 'Amy, I think you're letting the team down.'

'Huh?' Amy fiddled with the beads and wondered whether to slip the necklace on right now, even though it might look odd next to her delicate gold Tiffany necklace, the one she rarely took off because it had been a present from Damien when he first moved to London.

'You know. The WAG team! Didn't you say you'd spent yesterday at Barcelona's most exclusive boutiques with three of those fakes? But now look at you, buying cheap tat on the beach.' Asha was in full teasing mode. 'What would the WAGs think of that? Those beads are more plastic than *they* are.'

'You know it's all I can afford! I didn't buy anything at all yesterday. And those girls aren't plastic, or fake.' Amy thought about it. 'Well, Kylie's OK.'

Asha smirked. 'Yeah. If she only had a brain.'

'Now you sound like Trina!'

'Trina?' Asha pretended to think for a second. 'If she only had a heart. Ha – it's *The Wizard of Oz* for WAGs!'

Amy laughed in spite of herself, especially when she thought about what would be next in Asha's *Wizard of Oz* theme. 'Well, you can't tell me Lauren doesn't have courage. You should have seen the way she trampled all over Court-ney to get her man.'

'Yeah, Lauren's missing something else,' Asha said. 'Like a personality.'

'You're terrible.'

Asha grinned. 'Thanks.'

Susi arrived with ice cream and wanted to know why they were laughing, so Amy went into a long description of yesterday's shopping trip. It had taken hours of modelling by Kylie and loads of scathing comments by Trina and over-enthusiastic comments by Lauren, but eventually Kylie settled on a dress that was The One. It was loose-fitting satin, multi tiered and elegant. It looked frighteningly expen sive to Amy, but it was probably a fraction of the price Kylie had paid for the gold dress she wasn't going to wear after all.

After that, Trina decided they should hit the 'normal boutiques', each of which was filled with stunning designer creations. Everyone except Amy had piled into a taxi abso-lutely loaded with shopping bags at the end of the day.

'Did you manage OK?' Susi asked Amy, her eyes filled with concern.

Amy was relieved to hear Susi sounding more like her

usual self, even if it meant referring to Amy's old shopping addiction. 'Yeah. You know I'm completely recovered.'

Asha looked up. 'Yeah, except she just bought a necklace from some random passer-by.'

'He was a beach vendor! And it only cost two euros!'

'Two euros today, but you've got the taste for shopping again now,' Asha teased. 'Tomorrow you'll be hitting Louis Vuitton with your glamorous friends and spending two *hundred* euros on a belt.'

'No I won't! Anyway, you know it was never really an addiction. I just got swept up in things last summer.'

'Yeah. Must be a lot of pressure, being famous,' Asha mumbled, and it didn't sound like she was being sarcastic.

Amy was relieved when everyone let the subject drop. Asha seemed to have fallen asleep once more and Susi was perched on the edge of the lounger staring into the distance again.

Amy shrugged and finished her ice cream, watching the bright sunlight bounce off the glistening waves. Then she went for a long swim in the sea, her thoughts full of the fact that tomorrow she was going to watch England – and hopefully Damien – play against the Netherlands in their first match of the World Cup.

9

The atmosphere outside the stadium was amazing. Everything seemed bigger and brighter in the Spanish afternoon sunshine. Amy stood behind the line of security guards by the entrance to the VIP and press area. Various friends and family members of the England team walked past and she felt like giving up waiting for Trina and Lauren and running in after them. She was finding it hard to contain her pre-match excitement. Damien had been sending her text updates whenever possible. The last was this morning and it seemed highly likely that he would be playing today. He must have really impressed Joe Vulkan since he'd arrived. She hugged herself in the short cotton wrap she'd thrown on top of her red and white outfit. She was so proud of him.

A limo drew up and Trina and Lauren got out, clearly in the middle of what looked like a really heated discussion. They got past security and reached Amy, where she quickly worked out their topic of debate was shoes. Lauren was bragging about her latest purchases and Trina was giving compliments that were actually thinly veiled insults. Lauren had a wide smile plastered on her face and kept talking brightly even though she must have known what Trina really meant.

'Hey, Amy!' a different high-pitched voice cut through the shoe argument, and Amy looked over. Kylie was standing the other side of security, dressed down in a flowing black dress and a tight-fitting orange jacket, her hair styled into light curls and piled in a fancy up-do.

Lauren stopped smiling and turned her nose up. 'We can't talk to *her* today,' she said. 'She's wearing Netherlands colours! I'm surprised they even let her near this part of the stadium.'

'Honestly, Lauren, she's our friend!' Trina scolded her. 'My boyfriend plays for a rival team too.'

'Yes, but not *today*.'

'So next week I won't be allowed to stand near you before the match?'

'Well . . . no, you won't.'

Trina snorted a laugh. 'OK, I probably won't anyway, but I don't think *you're* the one who decides where I stand, sweetie. Maybe I'll watch the England–Ghana match with Amy, whichever team I support.'

Amy wasn't completely sure about that, but she didn't feel like having a row with Trina right now – or with Lauren for that matter.

'I'll just go and see what Kylie wants,' she said, excusing herself and making her way back past security.

When she got there, Kylie was all hugs and air kisses. Amy tried to ignore the cameras that immediately trained themselves in their direction. The press were just arriving and clearly taking advantage of a pre-match photo opportunity. But sometimes it was easier to pretend they weren't there and life was normal.

'Hi, Kylie. Everything OK?'

Kylie smiled broadly at the cameras before she turned back to Amy, instantly losing the smile. 'No, I'm a nervous wreck! You?'

'Yeah, me too. Well, a bit. I'm mostly just happy for Damien, though. It'll be a dream come true for him, if he plays.'

'Aw, I know! Good for him.' Kylie laughed. 'Even if it does mean he could be playing against Johann today.'

A group of England fans walked past and stared obviously at Kylie's orange jacket, and they didn't seem to be admiring Kylie's figure, either. One of them yelled a few insults about the Netherlands.

Kylie flinched slightly and then smiled like she didn't care. She waited until the guys had walked off before she said, 'Listen, Amy, I'd better get back to my side pretty quick, but it's great that I caught you. I was going to call you later, but I saw you here and got my driver to stop straight away! I wanted to ask you a huge big favour.' She widened her large blue eyes at Amy. Kylie was always very hard to say no to. She had pleading expressions that matched those of her pet pug.

'Is it about Poshie?' Amy asked. It usually was, with Kylie.

Kylie stumbled in her mid-heeled Marc Jacobs pumps in pretend shock. At least, Amy thought it was pretend. 'Wow, yeah, it is! How did you guess?'

Amy shrugged. 'So how can I help?'

Kylie lowered her voice. 'Well, he's still not happy at the villa. The other day when I got back, he was more jumpy than ever.'

'Oh no! Really?'

'Well, hopefully it's nothing serious. I mean, the staff in the main house are OK, but . . . I think Poshie might need a friendly face, you know. Someone he knows from England, someone who speaks his language.' She nodded at Amy. 'So I was wondering whether you could come and keep an eye on Poshie for me tonight? I know he loves you to bits, and I can't think of anyone else to ask. Everyone else I know is out, but I heard you weren't doing anything.'

Amy smiled to herself. Great – the news was out that she was the only person in Spain who had no social life. Even Asha and Susi had mumbled something vague about plans for later, and she'd been in too much of a pre-match rush to find out what exactly they were doing.

Kylie mistook Amy's silence for hesitation. 'It would just be for a couple of hours,' she wheedled. 'Johann's got this thing to go to. I'd turn it down – I know Poshie should come first – but it's the Netherlands' first match and the manager is expecting us there, and, you know, Johann's been so patient with the whole wedding problem, and it's his career . . .'

'Oh, you don't have to explain.' Amy thought again how lucky Kylie was that Johann's manager was allowing players and their girlfriends so much time together, unlike Damien's. 'So you just need me to dog-sit, right?'

Kylie gave a huge sigh of relief. 'Yeah. You don't have to do anything, really. Just, you know, be there and make sure Poshie's OK. You know where Rosay's villa is, don't you? Oh, wait, you're in the Hotel Madrid, aren't you? I can send a car for you and tell the staff to expect you. Thanks – you're a star.' She gave Amy another hug before she pulled back and admired her necklace. 'Hey, is that Yves Saint Laurent? I saw chunky beads like those in the autumn range.'

'Oh, no, this one's from . . . a different range,' said Amy, tucking it into the neckline of her top to hide it.

Some press got really close to them then, so Amy pulled out the Tiffany necklace from Damien instead, hoping it would get in their shots. She always liked to get that necklace in photos – it made her feel better about all the ridiculous gossip about her and Josh that was usually printed underneath.

'Oh, great. Well, bye, Amy, and good luck to both our boys, eh?'

'Yeah, good luck. Hope Johann has a good game,' she added politely.

Kylie smiled and darted away and Amy let herself be photographed for a while before she headed back through security.

A roar swelled in the crowd as Amy took her seat between Trina and Lauren. The players were arriving. Amy turned her attention to the pitch, her heart thumping. Any minute now, she could be watching Damien play for his country.

Amy left the stadium in a daze. The match had ended in a goal-less draw, but it had been nail-biting, with both sides shining on the pitch. And it was brilliant to see Damien, though he'd been mostly on the subs bench. He'd only played the final twenty minutes and he hadn't seemed totally sure of himself, but the important thing was that he'd played. Amy's throat was sore from cheering like crazy every time he got near the ball. Now she wished she could congratulate him, or at least speak to him. She knew it wouldn't be possible for ages, though. Even when he played for Royal Boroughs, she always had to wait a long time to contact him after a match. There was probably even more post-match stuff to get through now that he was playing at the very top level.

Amy sighed and tuned back into the voices of Trina and Lauren, which she'd been ignoring as much as possible over the past ninety-odd minutes. They were sitting in the plush Café Biarritz, which was in an elegant suburb of Barcelona filled with gated apartment complexes and luxury car dealerships. Amy sipped mineral water while Trina and Lauren planned a big night out and argued over which clubs and bars were the best and coolest.

'Stevie really rates this place called Las Lindas,' Lauren was saying. 'He said it has the best atmosphere.'

'You mean the best topless bar staff, hun,' Trina said.

'They have a revealing uniform, that's all! It's smart,' Lauren protested. 'Anyway, my Steve wouldn't look, not when he has me.' She stuck her chest out to prove her point.

'Not much!' Trina mouthed at Amy while Lauren was absorbed in checking her phone. Out loud, Trina said, 'I've decided we're going to Baila Baila. I fancy a classy place. Want to tag along, Amy? I heard you'd be on your own tonight.'

Where was everyone getting this news? Amy hadn't seen the British papers today – had the top headline been '*Amy Thornton has no life!*'?

'Oh, sorry, I can't come. I promised Kylie I'd help out

77

with Poshie. She's out with Johann and she wants someone to watch him.'

'Are you serious?' Lauren gasped, her mouth hanging open unattractively.

'Yeah. Why not? Kylie's a friend, and Poshie's a gorgeous dog.'

'You're spending the team's rare night off *dog-sitting*?'

Trina shook her head. 'Lauren, shut up,' she hissed. 'You're the one that told me about this earlier! Amy's on her own tonight, remember?'

Lauren clapped a hand dramatically over her mouth. 'Oops, yeah. Sorry,' she said insincerely.

Amy shook her head uneasily. 'But Damien can't go out tonight.' Surely Lauren knew that? 'Can he? At least, he didn't tell me . . .'

She stopped talking because she couldn't stand the knowing look that was passing between Trina and Lauren. After ninety-plus minutes of bickering, those two suddenly seemed united in something – sympathy for her. It was horrible.

'I mean, I must have forgotten . . .' Amy was sure she wasn't fooling anyone.

'Yeah. Course, Amy,' Lauren said kindly. 'You missed the *Daily World* this morning, then? There was a thing about how Joe Vulkan announced a "family day" for the team after each match. It had photos of all the England WAGs, and it called us "shallow" and "a drain on the world's resources".' She sounded quite proud of herself. 'They got a lovely shot of me in my most flattering Marc Jacobs trousers. And you in your functional *Absolutely Amy* cossie.'

'Oh. No, I haven't seen the papers,' Amy said. 'I was

working on the DVD all morning, until I came here. No one there mentioned it.'

It had been a strange day at the shoot, with the team still short-staffed, Jessie the producer flapping about desperately on the beach and Amy's best friends behaving weirdly. Though maybe Asha and Susi knew about Joe Vulkan's announcement and that was why they hadn't invited her along with them tonight? They must have assumed Amy would be out with Damien.

'So the whole of the England team's allowed out tonight?' Amy couldn't resist adding, even though she was telling herself to leave it now.

'Yeah,' Lauren said. 'Tonight . . . and all day tomorrow.' She sounded like she was *trying* to shock Amy.

All day tomorrow? Why hadn't Damien said anything?

Amy bit her lip. OK, she and Damien had been through things like this before. She knew he had to have a good reason for not having told her. Maybe he was planning to surprise her, or something.

'Ooh, you obviously haven't seen *Just Gossip*'s website today either,' Lauren said, a smile playing on her lips. 'I nearly asked you about it when you arrived, but then I thought I'd better not.'

Amy looked at Trina, but Trina just shrugged. 'I haven't seen it. I only know what Lauren told me. I don't read any of that rubbish, unless it's about me. I don't really know what Lauren's acting so smug about.'

'Why did you sound like you knew all about it when I told you then? And I'm not acting smug!' Lauren protested. 'I'd probably even be a bit jealous, if it wasn't for the fact that I have my Stevie. Who wouldn't want to be romantically linked to Danny Harris himself?'

'What?' Amy gasped. 'We were *romantically linked* on the web? Me and Danny?' It was a few days since that night at Rio Grande, which had to be the source of this gossip. Why was it coming out now? And when most of the people at the club were footballers and their friends, how could the rumour have reached *Just Gossip*?

'Yeah. It was another article about the England team seeing their girlfriends and families, and then loads of people left comments. Including someone who said that Damien wasn't going out at all, and someone else who said it was because you'd been spotted dancing the night away with Danny Harris. It said you'd probably be out with Danny instead of Damien.'

'*What?*'

'It was pretty shocking,' Lauren said smugly. 'And then another person said that Damien was staying in because he wanted to talk to Paige Young in rehab. *All night*, if you know what I mean. I mean, what *they* meant.' Then she made a sad face and said, 'Oh, sorry. I'm sure it's nothing to worry about.'

'Yeah, I'm sure you're right,' Amy said as casually as possible. Lauren was really tactless, and whether she was doing it on purpose or not, Amy wasn't going to give her the satisfaction of looking upset. She was already sure none of this was as bad as Lauren was making it sound. She and Damien had been through something like *this* before, too. In fact, they were still going through it. Amy had lost count of the number of times the press had suggested there was something going on between her and Josh. Damien always brushed it off. And hopefully he'd do the same now with the Danny rumours, if he'd heard them.

The fact remained that Damien hadn't told her that he had time off, though. And he'd been texting her loads, even this morning, which had to be after Joe Vulkan had announced his decision. So why hadn't Damien mentioned it?

A sleek black Mercedes pulled up outside the cafe.

'Here's our car.' Lauren stood up, throwing a generous wad of notes on their table. 'Steve's treat. Isn't he wonderful? You coming with us, Amy?'

'No, I think I'll . . .'

Lauren gave her a super-sympathetic look, which she underlined by simpering, 'Yeah, I understand. You've got a call to make, haven't you? Oh well, Trina and I are hitting some boutiques now. We need new outfits for tonight!'

'Well, yeah, Lauren does. I've already got some fabulous clothes, but I just fancy going shopping,' Trina remarked as she walked towards the car.

Lauren gave a tight smile and called, 'Bye, Amy! Hope you sort things out with Damien. Or Danny, or whoever you're going for now. Long as it's not my Steve!'

10

Amy waited until she was firmly settled in front of the giant television screen in one of Kylie's many luxurious rooms, with Poshie sleeping heavily in her lap like a cat, before she called Damien. This was partly because she knew that if Johann was already out, it was probably safe to assume that other footballers would be off-duty too.

It was also because before she called him, she'd wanted to find the website Lauren had talked about and see for herself exactly what she was up against. Just in case.

It had been a bit difficult to get online. First she tried on her phone, but it kept cutting out. Then she went to the lobby at the Hotel Madrid, where there was a line of computers and Wi-Fi for the use of guests. It was permanently busy, though, probably because half of the hotel guests were members of the UK media who were covering the World Cup.

Amy had sat in one of the oversized leather chairs and waited, hiding behind her shades as she watched the press at work. She tried hard not to think evil thoughts about them. How much easier would her life be if all the journalists in the world suddenly disappeared? Or maybe if they just left her – and Damien – completely alone. She thought back to the days when she'd first started going out with Damien in Stanleydale and their biggest problems had been begging their parents for enough cash to pay for a decent night out. They'd make it to Pizza Express in Leeds with their Saturday job money if they were lucky.

Now Damien could afford to take her to some of the most exclusive restaurants in the biggest cities in the world, but they were paying a different price. It felt like they were being watched all the time; like they weren't just Amy and Damien any more, two ordinary teenagers going out together. They were the property of magazines and gossip blogs. Everything they wore and said and did – and quite a lot of stuff they didn't do at all – was up for scrutiny by a bunch of journalists, and then by the whole of Britain. Amy had been pretty sheltered from it over the past year – going to school, living a normal life with her family in Stanleydale – but it hadn't really gone away. It had been waiting for her round the corner, ready to pounce. She sighed and picked up an English newspaper that had been abandoned on the table in front of her. She knew she needed exposure to sell her DVDs, and media interest was part of the package that came with Damien's dream job, but that didn't mean it was easy to cope with.

Then she looked at the paper and instantly felt a bit guilty for the way she'd been thinking. There was a photo of her on the front page, taken on her shopping trip with Kylie, Trina and Lauren, though the shot was of her alone. She was walking along and her hair had been captured mid-swish like something out of a shampoo advert. The caption read: '*Inside: The Real World Glamour of Amy Thornton*'. She flicked through and found the piece, which showed the four girls on their Las Ramblas shopping trip. In each shot, Amy was highlighted favourably in contrast to the others, with little circles showing things like '*outfit bought on high street*', '*shoes from catalogue*' and even '*naturally fit body*'. It concluded that Amy was '*an inspiration to girls every- where – a recessionista with a truly natural sense of style!*' Then there was a competition to win copies of her DVD.

After about half an hour, Amy finally got a seat at one of the computers. She looked up *Just Gossip* and scoured the site until she found the feature Lauren had been talking about.

Her heart pounded as she started to read, but her suspi- cions were confirmed quickly. It wasn't really that bad. As Lauren had described, there was an article about Joe Vulkan's announcement that he was giving the boys twenty-four hours off after each game. Then there were about a hundred comments, which were mostly along the lines of '*Goooo on, England!*', '*Away the lads!*' and '*Lol, wuddent say no to 24 hours wiv Danny Harris, he is HOTTTT!!!!!*'.

Then, further down, things got more personal. There was the message about Damien not going out at all, then the one about Amy having been seen dancing with Danny Harris and probably going out with him instead of Damien, and the part about Damien calling Paige Young. After that, a couple of people said that Amy didn't deserve Damien *or* Danny, and who did she think she was anyway? She wasn't even good-looking! Her hair was stringy and probably *dyed*! And she was selfish and money-grabbing and shallow!

Amy walked away from the computer and went back to

Kylie's, shrugging the whole thing off pretty easily. She realized that, on the whole, she was on good terms with the British media. She'd got off to a shaky start with the press when she'd arrived in London last summer, but Rosay had helped her out with that. Now most publications seemed to love her, plus she had a good PR agency, which meant there wasn't usually much negative stuff printed about her. People who posted on gossip sites were in the minority and she didn't really care what they thought.

It was time to speak to someone she *did* care about, though.

Amy stroked Poshie's fur absent-mindedly with one hand as she hit the speed-dial button with the other.

To her surprise, Damien answered on the first ring and said over-brightly, 'I was just about to call you, Ames!'

'Really?' Amy couldn't keep the note of suspicion out of her voice.

There was a silence.

Amy sank further into the white leather of the sofa while she waited for him to reply. She focused on a photomontage in a wooden frame propped above the fireplace. It held about five different poses of Kylie on nights out with Johann, and one of Kylie and her best friend Paige Young, their arms flung round each other, both smiling. Paige seemed healthier and more pink-cheeked than Amy had ever seen her look. It must have been an old photo.

Damien still wasn't answering.

Amy checked her phone hadn't cut out. 'Damien?'

'No,' he said quietly at last. 'You're right. I've been sitting here holding the phone thinking I *should* call, though.' He sighed, then added, 'Oh, Ames, I'm sorry, I really am. I didn't know how to tell you.'

'Tell me what?' Amy said, now struggling to stay calm. There couldn't possibly be any truth in any of the stuff she'd read, could there?

'I mean, about my time off.'

'Oh, yeah. That.'

'And how I'm not taking it.' He took a deep breath. 'I'm staying here for extra training and stuff. I'm really sorry. I want to see you, I really do –'

Amy felt a rush of anger. 'Is it because of Joe Vulkan? Isn't he letting you have time off? Why not? It's not fair! You were ace today!'

'Thanks, Ames, but you know I've played better.' He sounded really down. 'I don't know, I just . . . I don't feel ready, you know. I don't feel like I can take my eye off the ball for a second.' He gave a light laugh. 'Literally, you know. I don't want to risk getting distracted –'

'I wouldn't distract you,' Amy said indignantly. She thought a bit. 'Well, not if you didn't want me to.'

'Yeah, see . . . OK, I'd distract *myself*, being with you,' he said softly. 'I don't mean it nasty, Ames, I swear! You know what I mean, don't you? I just can't stop thinking about football, even for a day – I don't want to lose focus. I'm not like the others here. I feel like a little kid half the time. Joe Vulkan didn't even want me here –'

Desperation rose in Amy's throat. 'He did! He's the England manager, not some PE teacher trying to give every Year Seven a go at the ball! He called you in because you're the best.'

86

'He called me in as a last-minute replacement. Last choice.'

'No way! You can't think like that, Day!'

'Yeah, that's just it. I can't. I don't play at my best like this.' He sighed again. 'So if I build myself up with some extra training and things, you know – show Joe Vulkan I'm made of the right stuff . . . I mean, you saw the way he looked at me when I was with you the other day, Ames! I know it sounds stupid, but I feel like I started off on the wrong foot with him.'

'Because of me?'

'No. Yes. *No*, I mean if I can just show him I'm dead serious about it all . . . I'll be more sure of myself too.'

Amy swallowed hard.

'Ames? Is that OK? I'm really sorry.' He sounded like he meant it. 'I really wanted to see you.'

'I really wanted to see you too,' she said quietly.

'But can we just try it? Can we see how it goes? It's only a short while, a few weeks at the most, if things go well, which they should . . . But, you know, it's so important. You do understand, don't you?'

Amy blinked a lot and cuddled Poshie. 'Yeah. Yeah, I think so. But, Damien . . .'

'Yeah?'

'I thought . . . I thought we weren't going to do this any more. This not telling each other stuff, I mean. Why didn't you tell me yesterday, or this morning, that you had time off and you weren't going to see me?'

'I suppose I wasn't completely sure until after that match. And then . . . yeah. I was holding the phone to ring you just now, Ames, I swear. I was just thinking of the right words and stuff.'

'But everyone I spoke to today seemed to know! There were random people discussing it online before the game!'

'You're joking?' Damien sighed. 'God, Danny was saying the other day that he can't even sneeze without it getting reported somewhere. Well, great – maybe I'm more like him than I think.' It was obviously his attempt at a joke, but Amy didn't laugh.

'Day, you must have spoken to *someone* about it. Before me, I mean.' Amy wasn't sure why exactly she was insisting with this, but it just felt too weird that a rumour like that had started out of nowhere.

'Not really. I mean, I probably mentioned it last night after training, when Steve was talking about seeing his girl-friend and I said . . .'

Amy breathed a sigh of relief that made Poshie stir. 'Oh well, if you told Steve, then that completely explains it.'

In fact, when Amy thought about it, she realized Lauren might even have been one of the people who commented on the *Just Gossip* site. Amy wouldn't put it past her – Lauren used to run a blog that was all about WAG gossip. She was a real stirrer.

Damien didn't sound too shocked either. 'You think Steve's been talking to the press?'

'No,' Amy said. 'I think he's been talking to his new girl-friend.'

'I don't know what his problem is! The only thing I can think of is that it's because I got played and he probably won't – not while we have Alex Hills in goal. But Steve's been a total nightmare lately, always shooting his mouth off.'

'So has Lauren.' Amy thought that Courtney was well shot of Steve after all – compared to Lauren, she was way too nice for him. Lauren and Steve were as bad as each other! 'Why, what has Steve been saying?'

Damien replied tentatively, 'Well, he keeps going on about you . . . you and Danny, you know . . .'

Amy gasped. 'Oh no! Damien, honestly –'

'Don't worry, I know it's all lies, not least because he always shuts up the second Danny's in earshot. He's made up all this stuff about you and Danny clubbing all night and he thinks it's a great joke to go on about it.'

'Oh, yeah. I . . .' Amy gripped the phone, realising she was guilty of not telling Damien stuff too. 'I *was* with Danny in a club the other night. But there were loads of other people around and . . .'

'Oh, right.' Damien's voice was low. 'So it's *true*?'

'Kind of. But, Damien, it was that other time you didn't go out . . .'

'No, I understand. I do.' He sounded determined. 'You should still have fun. You just, you know . . . didn't mention it before.' He breathed in sharply. 'So . . . what are you doing tonight, Ames? Dancing the night away with my team captain again?' He gave a strained laugh.

Amy thought she'd try to make a joke of it too. 'Yeah, according to that website. And you're talking to Paige all night again, yeah?' She laughed.

Damien didn't. 'Is that what it said?'

'Yeah.' She hesitated. 'Why, is *that* true?'

'Well, definitely not the way that lot probably made it sound.'

'Oh. Yeah. Course.' Amy knew Damien and Paige were friends. He'd never mentioned that they were in touch right now, though, while Paige was hospitalized for a relapse in her eating disorder. 'Do you call Paige a lot, then? I mean . . .'

'Sometimes. Just when she has stuff she wants to talk through.'

'Oh.' Amy gulped. 'You never said.'

'She's been having a tough time of it, you know.'

'Yeah. Sure.' She just managed to stop herself adding: *so has Danny*. It would be spiteful, and pretty stupid.

But she'd still been tempted to say it. Really tempted.

After all, it was Damien's fault that she was at Kylie's house dog-sitting instead of out on the town with him. But he was too busy being 'focused' to see her. Though he still had time to call Paige Young.

She made a face at the photo of Paige and Kylie. Then something occurred to her. Kylie had known that Amy wasn't going out tonight. But she probably hadn't heard it from Lauren, who was making a huge point of not talking to 'rivals' on match day. Had she read it on the *Just Gossip* site, or . . . Had she heard it from her best friend?

'Damien, can I ask you something?'

'Yeah, course, Ames.' He sounded wary.

She knew she shouldn't say it. She and Damien had been through this! Amy was over it. *They* were over it. But she needed to get the thought out of her head. 'Did you tell Paige about how you weren't going to see me tonight? Did you tell her earlier?'

'I . . . Er, yeah. Maybe.'

'Maybe?'

'OK. Yeah, I think I might have mentioned it.'

'Right. So you told Paige Young what you were doing before you told me? When it affects *me,* not her!'

There was a silence. Then Damien said, 'OK. What exactly are you getting at?' He sounded like he was speaking through gritted teeth. 'You know, Amy, aren't you actually too busy filming with *Josh Hunt* tomorrow to see me anyway?'

'Oh my God! *Damien*!' Amy could not believe he'd said that. After all the times he'd insisted that none of the gossip affected him!

'Every magazine in the country has been full of *that* gossip for months! The lads are constantly taking the mick, you know. And now I have Steve on about you and Danny Harris too!'

'You always say you don't care! That it's all gossip!'

'Yeah, I know. But you're always moaning about the press, and then you play right into their hands by filming with the person everyone says you're seeing behind my back! And then being seen in public with Danny Harris! You're *giving* them stuff to write about.'

'Yeah? Well, I only came here to make a DVD! I was here first, and you were supposed to be in England. It's only since you arrived that I'm getting all this extra media attention!' Amy hadn't realized how loud her voice had got until Poshie sat up and leapt off her lap with a yelp. 'And anyway, what about *you*? You're calling the girl everyone says you have a thing for!'

'I'm not doing it in the public eye like you are! I talk to Paige in private. I have no idea how it got out.'

'Oh great. Yeah. In *private*. So private that you're telling Paige things you haven't even told *me*! And as for how it "got out" . . .' She took a deep breath as her hurt nearly overtook her anger. 'You sound like you really *do* have something to hide!'

Poshie ran to the patio window, yapping wildly.

'That sounds like Poshie!' Damien said. 'Is it? Are you with Kylie?'

'What's it to *you*? You looking for something to tell Paige?'

'No, I'm just proving my point! Do you have any idea what the papers would say if they knew you were with Johann Haag's girlfriend the night after a Netherlands–England match?'

Amy didn't think she really cared right now. 'No. What?'

'They'll say you're not on our side. It would get back to Joe Vulkan and –'

Poshie's yapping grew more panicked, echoing the way Amy was feeling. He ran out of the room in a frenzy.

'I don't think so! And Damien, you know what? I am *sick* of the way you're running scared of what your precious manager thinks! He's given you a day off and you don't even have the guts to take it, all because he looked at me funny – once! So now you'd rather play it safe by sitting in . . . and calling Paige!'

'You know it's not like that! I thought you understood! This is –'

'A huge opportunity?'

'Yeah. It is. It's the *World Cup*!'

There was a long, tense silence. Even Poshie's barking was more distant.

Damien broke first. 'Amy? Let's not . . . I don't want to row with you. I miss you! I didn't mean what I said. And you're right that I should have told you sooner about tonight and tomorrow, and Paige – she's just a friend. You know that, don't you?'

'Yeah. I know. I understand.' Amy sighed. 'Look, forget it. Poshie's legged it in a right state and I'm supposed to be looking after him while Kylie's out. I'll call you tomorrow. I mean, if . . .'

'Definitely call me.' Damien sounded really upset. 'And I'll call you too. Ames, honestly, I'm sorry. I love you. I miss you.'

'Yeah, me too. Night, Damien.'

She hung up and hurried out of the room in the direction that she'd seen Poshie take. She followed the distant yelping sound until she found herself in the luxurious reception room by the side entrance to Kylie's wing, where she found Poshie quivering in a corner. When the pug saw her, his yelping turned into whining, but he didn't move.

'God, I know the feeling, Poshie,' Amy said, walking towards him with her arms outstretched. 'But come on out. We'll be OK.'

The little pug just whimpered more.

Then Amy heard it. A chorus of fierce barking in the distance, getting closer. The villa's guard dogs were doing their worst. Amy had been relieved when the gardener had met her taxi at the gate and led her into the house tonight, talking sternly to the dogs to stop them approaching. At the party, the dogs had been held by the bouncers, but she knew that the rest of the time they more or less roamed freely in the vast grounds of the Di Rossi's property.

'Is that what's been scaring you, Poshie? Those big bad dogs?' Amy held her hand out to him. 'I'll have to tell Kylie . . . I mean, your mummy. She'll soon sort it all out, I'm sure. They need to keep those dogs on leads.'

Then she heard a male voice call out, and she froze.

Of course. The dogs probably had a good reason to bark like that. Maybe there really was an intruder. Amy's heart was in her mouth as she peered cautiously through the glass pane in the side door. For a while, it was too dark to see anything. Then an outside light snapped on and a stream of angry-sounding Spanish words instantly silenced the dogs. In the bright beam she saw the gardener standing with his hands on his hips, talking to . . . it was two people, standing by a greenhouse.

There was a man with his arms wrapped protectively round a woman. Amy stared. She opened the door a crack to get a better look, now she knew there was nothing to be scared of. She couldn't believe what she was seeing.

The woman was Rosay, which wasn't so surprising, seeing as this was her step-dad's villa. Kylie had assumed Rosay would be out, but maybe she didn't know for sure. And anyway, Rosay *was* outside. It looked like she might have been in the grounds for a while, too – or possibly in the greenhouse – as she had bits of plant life stuck to her otherwise perfect hair extensions.

The identity of the man – who had similar vegetation stuck to his jacket – was more of a shock. Amy hadn't seen him for ages and he looked slightly different. His hair was longer and he sported more of a rugged, half-shaven look. But he was still recognizable as the ex-heart-throb of the

Year 11 girls at Amy's school in Stanleydale. He was the footballer who'd fallen out of favour with the British public after last year's scandal, the ex-Boroughs striker who was held responsible by the media for causing Danny Harris's divorce. The guy Rosay was secretly in love with, but who she'd cruelly dumped anyway, partly so that Trina and the whole world wouldn't hate her.

Yes, he was definitely Scott White.

The gardener said something else to the dogs and they walked off with their tails between their legs.

As soon as they left, Poshie jumped into Amy's arms and yelped happily.

Rosay looked over, saw Amy and waved.

Scott White followed Rosay's gaze and gave Amy a look that was a lot like the one on the guard dogs' faces before they slunk away.

11

'Bloody dogs,' Rosay said to Amy as they lowered themselves into the soothing bubbles of the spa pool, either side of a spectacular cascading waterfall.

It was three days since Amy had spotted her with Scott White while Poshie-sitting, and they'd finally found a time when they were both free so that Rosay could tell her what exactly was going on in her life. Amy knew some of it now, of course, and she'd promised to keep it secret if Rosay explained the rest soon.

Rosay was just back from another singing-related trip to Madrid. And Amy had a day off from the DVD, basically because there had been one disaster after another with the shoot. The crew was back in full force, but they'd had problems with lighting and then with an unexpected summer storm. The owners of the beach area were now refusing to allow filming because of an important volleyball tournament that required the exact patch of sand allocated for the *Absolutely Amy* shoot. The producer had gone crazy, but the resort owners just shrugged and said it would only be a couple of days before they could have the space exclusively again.

Amy was secretly pleased. It was looking increasingly likely that she'd be able to stay for the next round of the World Cup. Josh, Asha and Susi seemed pleased too, though Amy hadn't seen them all that much. They had separate social lives right now. Amy got invited to a lot of parties and shopping trips by Kylie, Trina and Lauren, whereas Susi and Asha went . . . Amy wasn't completely sure where. She'd given up asking because they never gave her a proper answer. They always seemed to get home after her, though, and slept as much as possible in the daytime.

Meanwhile, Damien had been training hard and also ringing her a lot. They'd avoided the subjects of their argument; she'd told him all the problems at the shoot and he'd talked about England's chances at the game the next day. And at least this time she didn't expect to see him on the 'family day' she knew Joe Vulkan was allowing afterwards.

But right now Amy was at the most luxurious spa she'd ever been to – and after last summer with the WAGs, that was saying something. It was on the forty-second floor of a large hotel and it had amazing views over a craggy section of the Mediterranean coast. The churning bubbles inside contrasted with the back-and-forth rhythm of the waves they could see through the window, and Amy felt massaged and soothed. She'd always felt at home surrounded by water.

'So what's going on, Rosay?' Amy asked when they were settled. 'I can't believe you got back with Scott!'

Rosay swished her arm through the warm bubbles and sighed. 'It's been a crazy year. A couple of months ago, I decided . . . well, life's too short. So I looked him up. I thought he might not talk to me, but . . .' She shrugged. 'I think he's chilled out a lot, living in Spain and being out of the spotlight. He's like a different man.' Rosay went a bit red. 'Well, he's like the man I knew he was before, but no one else could see he was. If that makes any sense.'

Amy laughed. 'Wow, you've really got it bad!'

Rosay smiled sheepishly. 'I know. Sorry.'

'No, it's OK! He seems pretty crazy about you too.' Amy caught a bubble as it rose to the surface. 'I saw the way he was looking at you the other night.'

Rosay's smile broadened. 'God, it's good to talk about this to someone at last. You're the only person in the world who knows about Scott. Well, you and the gardener, and those annoying savage dogs at the villa. We thought we had it all worked out, you know, meeting in the greenhouse when Kylie and Trina were out! I smuggled Scott in when it was the dogs' feeding time and then after that, even if they barked outside, it was so far from the main house that we thought we could just ignore them. And it worked a couple of times, too, but then the gardener got suspicious!'

'Poshie was on to you as well,' Amy told Rosay. 'He was scared of the dogs and Kylie noticed him being jumpy after she was out. You were going to get found out sooner or later. You're lucky it was by me.'

Rosay nodded. 'Thanks for agreeing not to say anything. If the world found out, it would be disastrous for my album sales. Scott keeps telling me about how the press can make you or break you. But especially break you, he says.' She sighed. 'I'm not sure if I'm ready to be broken.'

They listened to the waterfall as it splashed into the pool.

Rosay was looking so sad that Amy said, 'Oh, hey. It can't

be that bad, can it? Can't your PR people help, and your dad?'

'Yeah, a bit. There's only so much they can do, really.'

'But you're not doing anything wrong!'

'I'm seeing Scott White, the guy who ruined the life of national hero Danny Harris! Everyone in Britain hates Scott. They're not really going to come round fast to the idea of us together.' Rosay moved to the edge of the pool and leant her head back. 'Mind you, the way I'm going with my fake relationships, I'm getting a pretty bad reputation all by myself! Though the edgy image isn't hurting the singing career.'

'It's not easy, is it?' Amy thought about all the pressures on her and Damien right now, and that almost-argument they'd had.

'You too? Come on, let's go to the next room and you can tell me all about what's going on in *your* life.'

They got out of the water, wrapped thick spa towels around their bikinis and headed for the wooden tranquillity of the sauna, where Amy told Rosay all about the non-stop Josh Hunt rumours, plus the new Danny Harris and Paige Young rumours, and her suspicions that Lauren Thompson had been stirring everything up online.

'God, I wouldn't put it past her!' Rosay said. 'Lauren's a nightmare! There was a party at mine just before we left for Spain, and she was right rubbing Courtney's face in it about Steve. Courtney got in such a state that I had to drag her to my room and talk her out of attacking anyone.' She rolled her eyes. 'And then she asked if I could leave her there to cool off, so I did, and Lauren actually went in when my back was turned to "patch things up". I can't decide whether she's clueless or cruel. Me and the housekeeper ended up throwing the pair of them out – separate exits, you know! Luckily, Courtney's sister whisked her off for some foreign holiday the next day and I think Courtney's still there right now, getting over her violent thoughts about Lauren.' Rosay put her feet up on the wooden bench and looked through the glass at the sea lapping on the shore. 'Oh, hey, that was actually the night I lost my phone! And you'll never guess what – the housekeeper found it the other day in the laundry room at the back of the house! Random, huh? I mean, I never go in there. Mum told me this morning.'

'Oh, where *is* your mum?' Amy asked idly. 'I haven't seen her.'

'No, she . . . She's at home in England. She's . . . not well.' Rosay's voice cracked. She bit her lip and looked away.

Amy sat up and scooted across the bench towards her friend. 'Oh no. What's wrong?' Her heart pounded at the memory of her own mum's cancer diagnosis the year before last. She was so relieved that her mum had the all-clear now, even though she still had check-ups, and moments when she felt very weak from all the treatment. Well, if Rosay needed someone to talk to about poorly mothers, Amy was definitely the right person.

'Just an operation she had. You know . . .' Rosay looked a bit embarrassed. 'Cosmetic surgery. Something went wrong and she needed longer to recover than she'd planned. In fact, she's needed a whole string of other operations to correct the bad one. She told us to go to Spain without her.' Rosay sighed and blinked a lot. 'It's like she always has to change *something* – her boobs aren't quite right, her eyelids need a tweak, and she's already had about five different types of facelift . . . I mean, she says it's all the outside pressure to look good, but I think a lot of it is just *her*, you know. Because when I look at her I just see my mum, but she sees something that needs *work*.' Rosay stared out of the window at the sea. 'She missed me singing at the opening ceremony because she was in surgery that day.'

'Oh, wow. Sorry to hear that,' Amy said. She managed to stifle the nagging feeling that Barbie di Rossi was bringing all this on herself – after all, maybe it was a kind of sickness, the way she kept having operations. Anyway, she felt bad that Rosay was suffering.

'Thanks. Oh, by the way, you don't need me to tell you that this is another massive secret, do you? Mum would hate it if this got in the papers, and Dad might even try to get hold of a picture or something, just to spite her. I haven't told him.' Rosay laughed bitterly. 'My life's one big lie right now. I've been meeting my secret boyfriend in a greenhouse, and I can't really go anywhere else with Scott because I feel like I have to stay near-ish to support my step-dad who's upset about my mum being secretly in hospital.'

Amy had to admit it sounded pretty messed up, even for Rosay, whose last few years had been filled with drama and scandal.

'So is your mum still in hospital?'

'She got out today. That's how I know about my phone. So, yay. One good thing, even though I have two new phones now.' Rosay forced a smile. 'Money's the only thing that's not a problem in my family. Oh, hey, remind me to give you one of my new numbers when we're in the relaxation suite at the end. And by the way, I'm paying for this whole spa day for both of us.'

'No, I . . .'

'You don't get a say in it!' She climbed gracefully down from the bench. 'Come on, all this heat's getting me down. Let's go to the ice fountain now.'

'The *what*?'

'You grab handfuls of ice flakes and rub them on your body. It wakes you right up. And after that we can get colour therapy if you fancy. And then we can start the treatments. Do you fancy a stone facial, or some Hopi ear candling, or should we just get pedicures?'

'Um . . .'

Rosay laughed. 'Trust me, by the time we leave this building, we are going to be totally stress-free!'

12

'I'm so incredibly stressed, it's untrue!' Asha was grumbling the next morning at breakfast. The hotel offered a large buffet, though Amy and the twins usually just grabbed apples on their way to the beach – Amy, because she'd been trying to swim in the hotel's mermaid pool; the twins, because they got out of bed really late; and Susi had never been keen on eating breakfast anyway. But today the shoot was still cancelled for the volleyball, and Asha and Susi had been woken up super early by a call from their mother. A call that made Asha rush down to gather all the English papers in the hotel lobby and tear through them while Susi loaded plates with a much bigger breakfast than usual for Asha and Amy, plus an apple for herself.

Asha held up the offending article. 'It's not fair! I didn't sign up for this. There should be a law against this kind of thing. In fact, there *is*, isn't there?' Asha was fully planning to become a high-flying barrister and Amy had no doubt that she'd make it. She was a genius in the school sixth form.

'Don't be such a drama queen, Ash,' Susi said. 'You know Amy's been dealing with stuff like this for ages now.'

Asha shook the paper indignantly, then held it still for Amy to look at it. At the top there was a photo of film star Rafael Badillo with his arm protectively steadying Asha as she climbed into a black Mercedes parked outside a restaurant in the city centre. It was in full colour, but it wasn't a very good shot. Maybe Asha had been in the middle of saying something, because her mouth was all twisted and her eyes were wide and she looked a bit . . . well, the worse for wear. It didn't help that the article said she was 'totally out of it'. It also called Asha a 'celebrity hanger-on' and said she'd had 'a tiny role' in a fitness DVD as a result of this.

'Mind you, the photos of Amy are usually way more flattering. I can't believe you're in the *Daily News* looking like that.' Susi shook her head. 'All our aunts and uncles read it.'

'Shut up! I know.'

'No wonder Mum wants you home on the next plane. You know what a hard time Uncle Dinesh gave her about letting us come out here in the first place – all that convincing him we'd be fully chaperoned the whole time.' Susi gave a wry smile. 'I don't think hot film stars were what Uncle Dinesh had in mind. Even if Raf-Bad did wear a dinner jacket.'

Asha made a face. 'Susi, *please* shut up! I don't know why you seem so happy about it. If I go home, you'll probably have to come too. Mum's never going to let you stay here without me.'

'She might. I'm the sensible one, remember?'

'It's not fair!' Asha ranted. 'Just because you never go out with *anyone*, ever, everyone thinks you're perfect!'

Susi shrugged.

'Anyway, I'll tell them you've been covering for me, and then you'll be in trouble too. What do you think of *that*?'

Susi narrowed her eyes. 'I think it's the last time I cover for you.'

Asha glared at her. Then she gave Amy an imploring look. 'Amy? What do I do? This is going to ruin my *life*!'

Amy tried to sound sympathetic, even though a little part of her was secretly a bit upset that Asha hadn't told her a thing about going out with Rafael Badillo, and Susi had been 'covering for her'. They could have told Amy – she was their friend!

But if Susi and Asha went home, what was going to happen to *Absolutely Amy*? Was it going to end up being just her and Josh? What would the papers say about *that*? Besides, even though her friends had been disappearing till all hours without telling her where they were going, she knew she'd really miss them if they went back to Stanleydale.

'I know. It's awful,' Amy said. 'But there's not much you *can* do. They print whatever they want to, more or less.'

'Yeah, what do you expect, Asha? I warned you about going out with him.'

Not in front of me, you didn't, Amy thought.

Susi seemed to realize it because she added, 'Yeah, sorry we didn't tell you, Amy. Asha and I decided we shouldn't, because the press were always hounding you. We thought it might cause trouble for you, if they started firing questions about Asha in among all the ones they usually ask you.' She bit her lip. 'Didn't help, though, did it? My sister managed to get herself papped anyway.'

'It was dark!' Asha protested. 'I didn't know there were photographers there.'

'Oh,' Amy said, trying to ignore the fact that she still felt hurt. 'Well, do you want me to speak to your mum about what a pack of lies they always print? I can give her loads of examples. I'm sure I can talk her round.'

Asha stared miserably into her coffee. 'You'd have to speak to our whole extended family – and good luck to you! They're much worse than my mum – and they already think she gives us way too much freedom. They also believe every word they read in the papers.' She gave a long sigh, gazing mournfully at the page. Then she did a little gasp and added, 'Though I don't know if they'd believe this nonsense about you supporting the Netherlands.'

Amy stared at her. 'What did you say?'

'It's right next to my thing. A picture of you and Kylie. Here.' Asha handed the paper over.

Amy looked away from the photo of Asha falling into a car and over at the facing page. There was a picture of her standing outside the stadium with Kylie Kemp. It was from the day of the first England match, when Kylie had asked her to Poshie-sit. But something about it looked different. She squinted closer.

Kylie was smiling at a string of beads round Amy's neck. A string of *orange* beads. The colour was all wrong. And Amy's outfit also looked like it had orange stripes on it too. The caption read: '*Has Amy switched sides and gone ORANGE?*'

She read a bit more. It suggested that Amy wasn't supporting England – that she'd secretly gone over to '*the other side*'. It also said that she had looked '*guilty*' when the cameras had caught her orange beads and '*hurriedly tried to hide the evidence*'. There was a small inset picture of her tucking the beads into her top, a huge orange arrow pointing to the incriminating section of the photo. It went on to say that Amy hadn't shown '*newest England recruit Damien Taylor*' much support in the last few days and that already she'd been 'linked with other men' since his arrival in Spain. Then it said that Damien and Amy hadn't been seen together at all, even on the '*Vulkan family day*'. There was a quote from '*a team member*' that confirmed this. The whole piece ended with a quote from '*a source close to the team*', which said, '*All I can say is that Amy Thornton might not be on our side and Damien should watch out!*'

Amy threw the paper down and put her head in her hands. The whole thing was so stupid! The red colour on the picture had obviously been doctored, and all the words were nonsense. Surely no one would believe it?

But it was annoying that Damien himself had told her the other day that he was worried about her being seen with Kylie Kemp as she might be accused of switching sides. She thought his suggestion then had been ridiculous, but now it turned out he was right. Was there no end to the traps you could fall into with the press?

'You OK, Amy?' Susi asked.

'Well, no one's going to believe *that*, are they?' Asha said, smiling at last. 'Yeah, actually, it could be perfect for convincing the family that my pic has been photoshopped too. This could be a lifeline. Who's coming back to the room with me for Operation Keep Asha in Spain?'

13

It hadn't gone well. The three of them had put Asha and Susi's mum on speakerphone and tried their best to talk her round, but Amy knew from growing up with the twins that once their mum had made up her mind about something, it was nearly impossible to get her to change it – ever.

After Amy's long speech about photoshopped photos, though, the twins' mum had caved a tiny bit and agreed to talk to the *Absolutely Amy* producer and find out exactly how much longer Asha and Susi would be needed. She said that if it was only a week or so, then they could stay. But there would be *no* more wild nights out for Asha, and if she saw *any* more photos like *that one* then she was coming over to drag her daughters home herself. Or if she couldn't get the time off work, she'd send Uncle Dinesh and he'd embarrass them so much they'd be begging to come home anyway.

Then she'd apologized to Susi and said she knew it wasn't her fault and it was a shame she was getting caught up in her sister's naughtiness again. Susi had looked a bit miffed at that, and Asha had smirked and whispered to Amy, 'Sometimes she forgets we're not six!'

After that, the three of them had sat around gloomily in

the hotel room. Amy tried to persuade her friends to go with her to the match, but Asha said she was too miserable and Susi made some excuse about needing to do some shopping.

As Amy was getting ready – taking care to dress entirely in the right colours – a text came through from Damien. She opened it excitedly, wondering whether he'd been told he was definitely playing. But all it said was: 'Lads saw paper! So stupid! xxx'

Amy was relieved about the kisses on the end – for a second she'd thought Damien was calling *her* stupid. But no, he obviously agreed with her that the article was ridiculous. So that was a relief – at least she didn't have to worry about telling him, or him hearing it from Steve, or anything like that. She texted back, agreeing, and then she told him how much she was looking forward to the match. She signed off with a row of kisses.

Damien didn't write again after that, but Amy knew he must be busy with all the pre-match preparation. She was doing quite a bit of it herself – she was determined to look her best. She went for indigo denim-look leggings and teamed them with a soft white tank and a tailored white jacket that couldn't possibly get her into any trouble. She made sure her Tiffany necklace was fully on show before she got to work on her make-up.

When Amy arrived at the stadium, Lauren was already in the family seating, leaning back to talk at the super-elegant wife of the long-standing England goalie Alex Hills. Lauren was dressed almost entirely in red, which made Amy frown. She saw Amy and called out, 'Amy, at last! I've been waiting for you!'

Amy sighed and took the seat Lauren had obviously saved for her.

'Thank God you're here,' Lauren leant over and whispered. 'That lot are so stuck up!'

Amy didn't really have a problem with the others – they'd always been friendly enough to her. She thought they probably just found Lauren very irritating. Right now, Lauren was looking her up and down.

'You're wearing Ghanaian colours!'

'I'm not,' Amy said, starting to panic. 'I'm wearing England white.'

'Not today. England are playing in their red away kit. Ghana's home kit is white. Did no one tell you?' Lauren laughed, smoothing down her gorgeous red silk top.

'No.' Amy's heart sank. But they were just white clothes! Surely it couldn't matter. She shielded her eyes from the cameras that were trained on her and tried not to think about it. Changing the subject seemed like a good idea.

'So, is Steve on today?' she asked. She knew it was unlikely. There were three goalies on the team and Amy was fairly sure, especially after what Damien had said, that Steve was Joe Vulkan's last choice.

'I don't think so, but maybe the next game! He's way better than the other two. Alex Hills is older than the *hills* now!' Lauren laughed heartily. 'Get it?'

The woman Lauren had just been talking to said something to the person sitting next to her and they both laughed cattily.

'See what I mean?' Lauren said quietly to Amy. 'I almost wish Trina was with us today after all. Even if I wouldn't have let her sit with us or anything, what with her boyfriend playing for the other side. But I've been texting her a bit. I don't think that counts as talking to the enemy, do you?'

'Oh . . . no. I'm sure it's fine.' Amy tried not to think about that newspaper article, or the fact that she really was wearing the wrong colours today.

'Guess what? I heard on the grapevine that Courtney's back. Do you think I should try to get in touch with her?'

Amy stared at her. 'Are you serious?'

Lauren nodded. 'I did think of ringing her before, while she was on holiday, but Trina told me that she didn't have a phone with her. She's back now, so I could call if Trina gives me the number – Trina has nearly all the girls' numbers, she's like a WAG encyclopedia –'

'Don't you mean phone book?' said Amy irritably. 'And do you really think Courtney would want to hear from you?'

'Yeah, why not? She left on bad terms with me because of Steve and all. But I think she just needed time to accept that her and Steve are over. She'll probably be OK with me now, won't she, after a break? I just want to make sure there are no hard feelings. I hate it when people don't like me, don't you?'

'Lauren . . .' Amy started, but she didn't know what to say next. *Are you crazy?* perhaps, or *I really don't think Courtney's going to forgive you that easily for stealing her boyfriend.*

'Oh, maybe you don't,' Lauren said. 'You seem to cope with it quite well. Wow, have you seen some of the stuff people are saying about you right now? Calling you a traitor, letting down your country? People on the *Just Gossip* blog are saying that Damien should dump you! They can't believe you'd wear orange to an England–Netherlands match.'

'What? But you saw me that day! You know I wasn't wearing orange!' Amy seriously could not believe Lauren.

'Yeah. But you're wearing white today, aren't you! So they'll be right if they say it today.'

'I didn't know,' Amy said indignantly. She thought about confronting Lauren about spreading nasty rumours. Then she decided to let it go. There was more important stuff going on. She sat back, tuned out Lauren's chatter and tried to focus as much as possible on the pitch, where the boys were about to arrive.

Damien's extra dedication must have paid off because he played right from the start of the match this time. It was amazing to watch him run up and down the pitch, so focused on his game. About ten minutes into the first half, Damien made a fantastic pass to Danny Harris, who promptly sent the ball flying into the back of the net. The crowd went wild as Danny celebrated and Amy wished she could run on the pitch and hug Damien, who'd been behind it all. He was an absolute star.

There were no more goals in the first half. Amy spent the start of half-time in a daze with Lauren wittering on beside her about how she was going to text Trina and all her friends and tell them about how Steve was way better than Alex Hills, and it was only because the rest of the England defenders were so good that Alex was shining in this match. After a minute or two of that, Lauren actually started texting and at least things went quiet.

Amy pulled out her own phone and sent happy messages to her mum and dad, who were sure to be watching this at home. Then she sent one to Damien, even though he was very unlikely to be anywhere near his phone right now. She just had to tell him how proud she was of him and how much she missed him.

She was about to put her phone away when the text message alert went off. It had to be her dad because she knew it couldn't be Damien.

But the display showed a number she didn't recognize. She opened it, puzzled.

It said: 'I have your number!!!'

Weird.

Lauren glanced over nosily. 'Oh, did you just get a message?'

'Er, yeah,' Amy said, feeling a sudden need to shield her phone from prying eyes, though she wasn't sure why.

'From Damien?'

'Er . . .'

'Because I just got one from Steve. I'm so sure he's not allowed to go sending me messages in the middle of the team talk – he's such a rebel! It's because he loves me so much, though. So what did Damien say?' Her eyes widened. 'Omigod, it's not from Damien, is it?'

'Er, no . . .'

'Is it from Danny Harris? It is, isn't it! Trina told me what Rosay said about how you two were looking on the dance floor! She said he has a thing for you. It is, isn't it? It's from Danny Harris!'

Amy looked at it and wondered. Could it be? After all,

she'd told him to contact her anytime. She started scrolling through her phone to compare the number to the one on the message he'd definitely sent.

But surely he wouldn't send her a text *now*? And anyway the message was extremely strange. '*I have your number*'? Well, how else would anyone be able to text her? It sounded like a joke.

Lauren chattered on. 'And yeah, Steve was saying this morning that Damien was staying at Villa Dorada for the whole of family day again. He wondered if Danny would be seeing you instead!'

Amy looked up. 'Lauren!' She could not believe her, she really couldn't. She really hoped that Steve hadn't been saying things like that to Damien again, too.

'What?' Lauren widened her eyes innocently. 'I'm only saying that's what Steve said. And honestly, the look on your face! Total guilt!' She nudged Amy.

Amy gritted her teeth. She found the text she thought was from Danny Harris and opened it to double check. It showed his number at the top, and it was completely different. So there! He'd only sent her one message, right after that night at the club. The message just now was probably a wrong number. She wouldn't worry about it.

Then she realized Lauren was reading the message over her shoulder. 'Thx. Danny x,' it said.

'This message was from another time,' Amy explained quickly. Then she realized that didn't really help her cause. 'I mean, from the night at the club. After he took me back to the hotel.' Oh no. That sounded a hundred times worse.

Lauren was gazing at her in admiration. 'Ooh, Amy!'

'Lauren, no . . . honestly,' Amy tried one last time. 'He was just thanking me for being a friend.' But sounded a bit pathetic even to her, and anyway Lauren had gone back to alternately texting and giggling, and she didn't seem to be listening any more.

The England boys got off to a bad start in the second half. There was a string of mistakes in the defence, which led to Ghana having several promising shots, the last of which ended in a spectacular goal.

Lauren turned to Amy and gloated, 'See what I mean about Alex Hills? Steve would have easily saved that.'

Amy gritted her teeth as Alex's wife glared at them. She felt like standing up and declaring, 'She's not with me!' Instead, she said loudly, 'I'm sure England will get one back now!'

Thankfully, the action after that moved to the other side of the pitch and Amy watched Damien closely as he played. He seemed to have lost some of the confidence he had in the first half, and Amy made sure she cheered super-loudly if he got anywhere near the ball. Because of the way the other Group B games had gone, she knew a draw wouldn't be the end of the world (or the tournament) for England, but it wouldn't be a good thing, either. If England drew they'd have to fight extra-hard in their next match because they'd almost certainly need a win to go through. But if they could win today, their position would be pretty strong.

The fans grew quiet as the remaining minutes ticked by surprisingly quickly and there was no sign of a goal. But with seconds to spare, just when everyone seemed resigned to a draw, Damien won the ball in an amazing tackle, and he was pretty far forward. He was onside, too! Amy cheered like crazy as he headed for the goal and . . . was fouled, right in the penalty box.

The crowd went wild. There was a pause while the referee made his decision and then preparations were made for a penalty. A penalty that Damien was clearly going to take, judging by the movements of the team on the pitch.

Amy gripped Lauren's arm.

In the next few moments, Amy felt like she was in a vacuum. She could hardly breathe. Everything about her, and everyone around her, was focused on rectangle of green and a blur of red and white. Her boyfriend was on the brink of winning the game for England.

Damien ran to the ball, faltered slightly, then walloped it, so it went soaring . . .

Right over the goal.

It hadn't even come close.

Damien put his head in his hands and several team members, including Danny Harris, crowded around to pat him on the back.

There was a stunned silence from the England supporters before the crowd erupted into a cacophony. In no time at all, the whistle blew for the end of the game, and that was it. England had drawn with Ghana, a team Amy knew they'd really expected to beat.

But they'd come close to winning, thanks to Damien.

And then they hadn't made it, also because of Damien.

Amy bit her lip and filled up with worry. He was going to be devastated about this

She had to see him.

14

Amy hesitated by the gates of Villa Dorada and checked the time on her phone. She knew the guys were free now because Lauren had told her five hundred times exactly which fancy restaurant Steve was taking her to tonight and exactly when. She didn't have to feel nervous about approaching security and asking for her boyfriend. She was allowed to see him, after all. The boys had twenty-four hours off now.

And Damien obviously had too much pride to admit it – he wasn't answering his phone, but he'd sent a quick text with 'Am gutted. Can't tlk now. Rly sorry. xxx' in response to the ten reassuring messages she'd sent him, and he hadn't replied at all to the one she sent after that, the one that said, 'Can I come over?' But Amy had a feeling he needed a surprise visit from her anyway. She'd cheered him up after other defeats, hadn't she? And his team hadn't even lost this time. She knew she could talk him round.

The security guard in the peaked cap hadn't noticed Amy yet. He was sitting in his booth, chewing a pen and staring at the puzzle magazine he was holding up. In front of him were screens showing CCTV footage of Villa Dorada from various angles. Amy wondered where Damien was and wished she could skip this step and beam herself into the house to be with him right this second.

She took a deep breath and was about to announce herself to the security guard when her phone beeped.

It was a text from same number as before – the one she didn't recognize.

Well, maybe this time she'd work out who it was. She opened the message.

This one made her gasp. It said: 'Go home! He does not want you here! NO ONE DOES!'

Her heart thumped. This one didn't sound like a joke. Also, it really seemed to apply to her. What was going on?

Amy looked around, half-wondering whether anyone could see her there. Was this person saying Damien didn't want to see her? But who would do a thing like that, and in such a horrible way? From a number she didn't even recognize?

Should she ring them back? Or maybe text them? She felt like crying. But it was stupid – she decided to ignore it.

She cleared her throat and the security guard looked up from his crossword.

'I've come to see . . . Damien Taylor,' she said, in a much smaller voice than she'd planned. 'My boyfriend, Damien. I'm his girlfriend. He's not expecting me, but he'd want to see me, I know he would.'

The man gave her an odd look and picked up his phone.

A member of the Villa Dorada staff met Amy at the gates and led her through the maze-like marble-floored corridors, talking all the way about how the house was deserted and even Joe Vulkan had gone out for a change. 'Only one remains,' the woman remarked as she opened a door and motioned inside, before nodding and walking away.

The room was filled with leisure equipment and the air vibrated with loud rap music coming from a speaker in the corner, right by where Damien was standing, cue in hand and with his back to the door, leaning over a full-size snooker table.

Amy hesitated in the doorway and listened to the clinking as he made shot after shot on the purple baize, in time with the beat of the music. When he turned to change angles, Amy saw that his face was a mask of concentration, as if his life depended on potting the next ball. Damien had always been the kind of guy who threw himself into sport when he was upset.

He looked up and saw her, and for a second his expression didn't change. Amy gulped, wondering if she'd done the right thing coming here. Maybe he needed to be alone. Maybe he was angry with her about the 'orange' article after all, and the inevitable follow-ups that would be printed about her wearing the wrong colour today.

Then Damien's eyes lit in a disbelieving smile. He put the cue down and said, 'Amy, you're *here*? Wow! I didn't know you were allowed into this part of our fortress.'

Amy didn't know whether she was either, but she'd asked the security guard and here she was, so . . .

'I wanted to see you,' she said, walking over. 'I know you said . . . you know, you didn't want to see me, and I do respect that, but I thought, after today –'

Suddenly he was right in front of her, sweeping her firmly into his arms. He held her and kissed her hungrily, his hands in her hair and his mouth hot against hers.

'God, I've missed you, Ames,' he muttered before he shut his eyes and kissed her again, over and over, so that there was barely a gap for her to say, 'Me too.' All her worries melted away. Even that threatening text felt like nothing now. She was with Damien and everything was perfect.

They kissed until the track ended and the room was filled with silence.

Damien spoke first, his breath short and warm on her face. 'I still can't believe you're here. This is the best thing that's happened to me all day. I can't get over what I did! It was so incredibly *stupid*.'

'Damien,' Amy said quickly, her voice still trembling slightly from the kissing. She steadied her breathing and took a step back so she could see him properly. 'Don't blame yourself.'

'Who else can I blame? I messed it up, Amy. We could have sailed through to the second round, maybe even come top of the group. Now we have a fight on our hands, and depending on how the other games go, it's probably a battle for second place!'

'So you'll beat them and you'll get through and win all the other matches. I know you will, Day! You're ace! You were great out there today.'

He raised his eyebrows at her. 'Are we talking about the same match? I went to pieces out there! I totally bottled it.'

Amy reached for his hand and held it tightly. 'It's not *your* fault. It's a team game, right?'

He sighed. 'Yeah. Doesn't change the fact that I lost the

game . . . for the team.' His dark eyes burned with disappointment. Damien could be so intense. It was one of the things Amy loved about him. He never did anything without being completely involved in it.

But maybe he was taking it too far. 'Do you want to go out somewhere, Day? With me, I mean? We should go out! Barcelona's got some brilliant nightlife. You weren't really doing anything football-related just now anyway.'

A look of panic crossed his face. 'Ames, I can't. I might be just messing around right now, but I have to have an early night and do extra training tomorrow. I've got to improve my game. You saw what happened out there! I can't risk that happening again.'

He moved away from her and she was seriously worried that he was going to tell her to leave, for the sake of his game.

'But, Damien, I think you need some proper time off!' She knew she was right, but he didn't look like he was going to listen to her. Desperation made her add, 'Everyone else is out, aren't they? With their . . . you know. Wives or girlfriends. For the next twenty-four hours, like Joe Vulkan said. He wants you to have a proper rest, Damien! Even the team captain is off out somewhere, probably!'

She didn't mean it to sound like an accusation – or, at least, it hadn't started out that way – but Damien's eyes flashed.

Then he looked away. 'Oh, right. *Who* exactly do you want to go out with?'

She narrowed her eyes. 'You, of course,' she told him.

His voice was low. 'That's not what I keep hearing. Steve

was on about it again in half-time, you know. It made it hard to focus afterwards.' He walked over to the table and picked up the snooker cue, as if that was the end of the matter.

But it really wasn't. Amy followed him. '*What* was Steve on about?' she asked, though she sort of knew the answer and she dreaded hearing it again. It had been bad enough when she was at Kylie's house, talking to him on the phone. Now she could see the hurt he was clearly trying to hide, and it made it all a hundred times worse. But they needed to talk about it – she knew from experience that it was no good pretending everything was fine when it wasn't.

Damien avoided her eyes and potted a ball before he said, 'You know . . . you. You and Danny Harris.'

She moved to take his hand again, or maybe put her arms round him, but he positioned himself on the other side of the table for a shot. Or maybe to get away from her.

Amy felt a bubble of annoyance start to rise in her stomach. 'There's nothing going on with me and Danny Harris, and you know it,' she said. Then her indignation increased as she realized fully what Damien was getting at. 'Wait, are you saying Steve threw you off your game with some stupid gossip that you know isn't true? Are you blaming that rumour about me and Danny for what happened today on the pitch?'

Damien rested the cue on the table and looked at her. 'No, that's not what I'm saying. I know it was my fault I lost concentration. Not Steve's, not yours, not Danny's. Mine. OK, I don't really understand why Steve thinks it's so funny to go on about you and the team captain, but that's just how Steve is. He likes making those kind of jokes. He's always been like that. You should hear . . . never mind.'

'No, what? Come on, tell me.' Amy put her hands on her hips. 'I want to hear this.'

'I was only going to say . . .' Damien trailed off, but then he looked at her and seemed to reconsider. 'I was going to say that you should hear the way he talks about you and Josh Hunt, and he has done for ages. About the stuff he says you do with him. And –'

'Damien!'

'OK, I won't say any more than that – but you did ask! Anyway, honestly, I've worked this out now. It's just him. It's the way Steve is. It's because he thinks everyone's like him. He was seeing Lauren when he was still with Courtney – well, as you know . . .'

'I didn't know that! He was seeing both of them at the same time?'

Damien gave her a disbelieving look. 'Of course he was. I think he probably still would be, except for the fact that Lauren's here and Courtney's been off somewhere on holiday. And there have been other girls too.'

'Really? Other girls?' Amy found herself feeling sorry for the super-annoying Lauren, who probably didn't know a thing about this.

'Yeah, but that's not the point. I'm not trying to spread gossip, Amy. What I'm trying to say is that's all Steve thinks about. I've decided not to listen to him. But you know, I was kind of upset by *someone* on the team today. Someone who's not like Steve. You know . . .' He glanced around as if to make sure they were alone, even though he knew they were. The house was deserted. 'Danny Harris.'

'But he's your team captain! You think he's great. You've always said!'

'Yeah, exactly. He *is* great. I have loads of respect for him . . . as a footballer. And, like I said, I'm not blaming him. I know it's my fault. But my game did fall apart a bit when I'd just been thinking about what he's up to with . . . with . . .'

'Damien?'

He wouldn't look at her. 'With you,' he finished at last. 'I don't think Steve's making all of it up. He said Josh was after you, and it was true. I know you didn't do anything about it, but . . . you know. Josh did ask you out.' He took a deep breath. 'So, well, the fact is, Danny's single. And you told me he *did* dance with you all night at that club –'

'He was being friendly! I swear that's all.'

'Could you swear *he* sees it that way, Amy?' He sighed, put the cue down again and walked over to Amy. 'Because you are *amazing*. He'd be crazy not to want you. And it was that thought that kind of, you know . . . got to me.' He wrapped his arms round her.

As long as they were standing like that, Amy couldn't resist kissing Damien's neck.

He sighed, leant into her and stroked her hair, shutting his eyes. 'See? Crazy,' he repeated, with a catch in his voice. 'No wonder he texted you at half-time.'

Amy pulled back. 'Who told you that?' But she had a feeling she knew.

'Steve. He showed me a text from Lauren about it.'

So much for feeling sorry for Lauren! Amy wanted to kill her now.

'It's not true, Damien. Danny didn't text me today. Lauren thought he did, but she was wrong. I can't believe Steve showed you that just before you were about to go on for the second half!'

'It doesn't matter, Ames,' Damien said miserably. 'Like I said, it's *my* fault I lost it. I need to work harder. I need to improve my focus, remove myself from all distractions.'

Amy didn't like the way it sounded like he wanted to remove himself from *her* – or from caring about her.

But she managed to stop herself saying that. She knew this was a strange time for Damien. And he was so upset about what had happened today. She should try to understand.

'Do you . . . want me to leave, Damien?' she asked.

'No. Yes.' Damien stared at the snooker table. Then he looked up, his eyes deep and earnest. 'No. I want to spend the next twenty-four hours with you. At least.' He gave her a sad smile. 'But I can't, because I need to train tomorrow. I told Joe Vulkan I would. And I need to think things through. I need to stop today ever happening again. Do you know what I mean, Amy? I'm so happy you came to see me . . . but please say you understand?'

She was almost tempted to say she didn't. That there was no reason they couldn't at least have a night out, or a coffee tomorrow, or *something*. That being apart like this could only be bad – for both of them. It was the reason she'd ended up dancing with Danny Harris. It was the reason the latest rumours had taken hold.

More importantly, she wanted to be with him! And didn't he want to be with her?

But his eyes pleaded with her, with that dark intensity, and she sighed. 'Yeah, I understand. So . . .' She turned towards the door. 'So I'll go now, OK?'

'No.' He caught her arm and pulled her to him. 'Not yet,' he said.

She kissed him and the rest of the evening melted away.

15

It was only when Amy woke up in her hotel bed the next morning that she realized she'd forgotten to tell Damien about the strange text messages.

Well, maybe that was the end of them anyway. They were vaguely creepy – especially the second one – but it had to be some kind of joke, or wrong number or something. Amy hoped she wouldn't be getting any more.

The twins had been on their best behaviour since yesterday's call with their mum. Or rather, Asha had been, because Amy doubted that Susi had been getting up to anything anyway – she'd probably just been going out late with Asha to look out for her. Last night, when Amy got back pretty late from Villa Dorada, they'd both already been asleep. Now they were actually up before her, making a racket as they got ready for their first day back at the *Absolutely Amy* shoot after the break they'd had for the volleyball tournament.

Susi was especially bouncy, and by the time they got to the beach, Amy was feeling tired just from being around her.

They were in make-up in the canopied area of the resort

when Jessie, the producer, dressed in head-to-toe black Dior, approached Amy and said, 'Can I have a word? In private.'

'Oo-ooh!' Asha mouthed as soon as Jessie's back was turned, making it look like Amy was in trouble. Amy made a face at her. Though Asha was probably getting her own back for the many times Amy and Susi had mouthed similar things at her at school. Out of the three of them, Asha was the one who got told off most and put in detention. Amy had only been in serious trouble once, when she skipped a day to watch Damien's important tryouts. And Susi never even got spoken to sternly, ever. She was the perfect student with a shiny halo.

Despite Asha's taunt, Amy wasn't really worried as she followed Jessie into the bar area. This was probably about the production schedule or something – or hopefully about the way it would be extended and she could stay for Damien's later matches. She sat down at the bar opposite the producer and smiled.

Jessie didn't smile back. 'We have a serious problem,' she said.

'Oh?' Amy immediately thought of the phone call with Asha and Susi's mum the day before. 'Is it about the twins having to go home? Because I really think their mum's going to be OK about it now, and –'

'Yes, that was all sorted yesterday. It's not about the twins,' Jessie interrupted, still not smiling. It was starting to unnerve Amy. But not as much as when the producer added, 'It's about you.'

Amy stared at her in disbelief. 'Me? Why?'

Jessie flinched slightly. 'Have you seen the papers today, Amy?'

'No, we came straight here. What's the problem? Are they complaining that I wore white yesterday? Honestly, it's just a colour!' She sighed. 'They're always printing all kinds of rubbish.'

Jessie's expression hardened. 'It might be rubbish, Amy, but it's to do with your image. And your image is important for sales of this DVD. In fact, it's everything.'

Amy went all hot and cold. Jessie's tone was scaring her. 'What do you mean?'

Jessie frowned. 'I mean, my bosses are putting pressure on me here. The shoot is taking too long, with all the hiccups, and we are haemorrhaging money. Money we're unlikely to get back, if this continues.'

'If what continues, exactly?' Amy said through the pounding in her ears. She couldn't believe this was happening. What could the papers have said about her – what could be so bad? Surely no one was seriously worried about the team colour thing, and the rest was all just silly gossip.

'I've got a couple of the articles here if you want to see them,' Jessie said, digging into her large black messenger bag. 'But basically, it seems you're falling out of favour with the public, and fast. Your name is trending on Twitter, Amy, and not in a good way. The whole of England is blaming you for the disappointing result yesterday.'

Amy's laugh came out sounding really shrill. 'But you know that's ridiculous, right?'

Jessie just looked at her.

'How can it be my fault? I'm not a footballer, or a manager, or whatever! And I was there supporting the team

– cheering them on!' *Whatever colour I was wearing*, she added silently to herself.

'All I know is that there's definitely a backlash against you. And once it starts, this kind of thing usually gets worse.' Jessie pulled the papers out of her bag and laid them in front of her. 'Take a look,' she said. 'And have a word with your PR company if you can – see if they can claw things back for you a bit. We'll keep going for now, but if I get orders to pull the plug, then I have to do it.'

'But the World Cup tie-in footage!' Amy said, feeling desperate. 'What about that? We haven't even started filming it! And what about Josh and Asha and Susi – *they* haven't had any bad press!' Well, Asha had, but Amy realized she'd better not remind Jessie of that right now.

'I'm sorry, Amy. It's *Absolutely Amy* – you're at the centre. And if you're out of favour, then, you know, our sales plummet faster than you can say "bargain basement". That's the way the world of celebrity works. And our production company isn't the healthiest it's ever been, you know. They're talking about cutting their losses.' Jessie sighed. 'It's pretty bad for me, too, you know. All these weeks of working on it, and all the preparation before we left.' She got up, slinging her messenger bag over one shoulder. 'Listen, I'm going to apprise the others of the situation now. I just wanted to tell you first.'

After Jessie left, Amy stared miserably at the papers in front of her. She wasn't even sure she wanted to know what they said this time.

Then she took a deep breath and started flicking through the first paper in the pile.

She didn't have to look far. It was in the first few pages, right there with all the proper news. A massive photo of her leaving Rio Grande with Danny Harris, shielding her eyes as if she had something to hide, when really she was just reacting to the flashing lights in her face. A headline saying '*Amy loses it for England!*' A big quote from '*sources close to Danny*' saying how hurt and vulnerable he was right now, and how Amy was '*taking advantage of that*'. Then something about the effect Amy's actions clearly had on '*young DAMIEN TAYLOR (19) in yesterday's match against Ghana*'. It ended with: '*Is Amy deliberately sabotaging England's performance?*'

The next paper had her on the front cover, wearing white, sandwiched in between pictures of Damien and Danny in their away kits. That one said: '*Whose side is Amy on? NOT ENGLAND'S!*'

The last paper that Jessie had left included an opinion column about WAGs and how they shouldn't be allowed in a World Cup country at all. It managed to trash most of her friends – including, she was almost happy to see, Lauren Thompson – but then it ended with a stream of poison about Amy. She was '*set to ruin England's chances*' and '*her charm had worn thin*' and Joe Vulkan shouldn't allow her anywhere near his players – any of them.

Amy put the papers down and reached into her bag for her phone. She wanted to ring Damien – she wanted him to reassure her that she wasn't single-handedly responsible for ruining England's chances of World Cup victory. But she realized how selfish that would be, especially right now when Damien was busy blaming himself. And training. She couldn't interrupt that. That could be seen as deliberately trying to sabotage things, just like the articles said.

She thought about ringing her dad instead, but he'd be at work right now, and probably not half as proud of his daughter's boyfriend as he usually was. His mates were sure to mention Damien's penalty yesterday. A lot of them also read these papers. Suddenly Amy felt so irrationally ashamed of herself that she couldn't even bring herself to ring her mum, who was the only person guaranteed to be on her side. Instead she piled up the offending papers for Jessie, put her phone back in her bag and headed back to the set.

When she got there, Susi and Josh were talking quietly on the sand and Asha was alone in make-up, her face looking streaky as if she'd been crying. The make-up artist fussed around her looking like *she* wanted to cry.

'Oh my God, Amy!' Asha said, the minute she saw her. 'How could you do this to me? I don't want to go home! What am I going to tell Raf?'

Amy didn't feel like dealing with Asha if she was going to be like this. 'Can't he hop in his private jet and see you in Stanleydale?'

'Do you think he would?' Asha said and then her face darkened. 'Oh, you're kidding, aren't you? You think you're the only one who's good enough to have a celebrity boyfriend – or two!' She turned away.

Amy put a hand on her friend's shoulder. 'Asha, please tell me you don't believe that stuff.'

Asha shrugged, not looking at her.

'Come on . . . we'll figure something out.'

'I thought we'd already sorted something out, after all

that drama yesterday with my mum. I thought she'd get over it and we could stay even longer. But now it looks like it's going to be all over in a couple of days, if not sooner, because of . . . because of your selfishness!'

Amy felt a bubble of anger rise inside her. 'Why are you calling me selfish? I've barely seen you in the past week or so! I've been stuck on my own while you've been disappearing every night without me!'

'Oh don't you try to guilt-trip me! You've been off with all your shallow WAG friends doing glamorous things – and that's when you haven't been two-timing Damien!'

'You *know* that's not true!' Amy kicked at the sand. 'Oh my *God*, Asha! How is it that just yesterday I was supposed to sympathize with that pap shot of you, and today you're suddenly acting like what the papers said about me is fact?'

Asha flinched away from the make-up artist's fussing hands. 'I haven't even seen the papers – all I know is what Jessie told me. And it sounded pretty bad. Bad enough to get us all sent home any day now. Also, yeah, thanks for reminding me about the paps. Because it doesn't really matter what the world thinks of me, does it? I'm just a '*celebrity hanger-on*'!'

'What are you saying, Asha?'

'I'm saying we're completely different. That shot of me was unfair – I'm just a normal person. But you – you're in the spotlight! You're *asking* for this kind of exposure. And now you're abusing it just to get yourself more publicity – and you're just ruining *everything*.'

'Abusing . . . what?' Amy couldn't even look at Asha any more. 'Do you think I got any of that media coverage on purpose? Do you think I *want* people to accuse me of not supporting Damien?'

Asha didn't answer.

Amy's voice rose. 'Right! That's it. I am not talking to you about this – or about *anything*, actually, Asha – until you apologize to me! Because what you're saying is *way* out of order!' Amy stood, breathless with anger, and waited.

'Yeah, sorry, whatever,' Asha mumbled like she didn't mean it. The make-up girl busied herself with some blusher, pretending she wasn't listening.

'Susi?' Amy called in desperation. But Susi was still deep in conversation with Josh and she probably hadn't even heard a word of the argument. Susi was never there for Amy these days either! The twins were as bad as each other right now. Amy's eyes suddenly filled with tears. She expected her football-related friends to be self-obsessed and flighty, but not her solid-as-a-rock friends from home. When exactly had she lost them? She wasn't sure. All she knew was that, right now, it felt like she had no friends at all! The wavy line between the sea and the sand blurred before her in the distance. She blinked hard.

Jessie walked over from the other side of the beach. 'Are you ready for the shoot, guys?'

The make-up artist said in a small voice, 'I might just need to touch up Amy's eyes.'

16

It was the weirdest shoot ever. After five minutes Jessie suggested Susi should do the advanced steps because she seemed more enthusiastic than Asha right now. Apparently it was a suggestion Josh had made a while ago, but now Jessie could see what he'd been getting at. They were filming a different segment of the workout today and were still at the rehearsal stage with it, so in some ways it didn't matter, but Jessie seemed to think the twins could pass for each other anyway. She went as far as saying that, since the twins were identical except for Asha's longer hair, no one would notice they'd switched places if the stylist made some adjustments.

Amy was sure her friends would object to that – they didn't consider themselves remotely identical and they resented anyone who suggested otherwise.

But Josh made some comments about how perfect that would be, and Susi walked over with the same bounce in her step that she'd had all morning, even after Jessie's news. And Asha shrugged and trudged to Susi's spot like she wasn't bothered either way. As the stylist gave her a quick up-do that would match Susi's from a certain angle, Amy felt like snapping at Asha – if she was so super-keen on staying in Spain, why was she being like this, causing trouble on the shoot with her attitude? Asha was in such a grump that she wasn't even bothering to make her usual quips about Josh today! Amy almost missed them. No, she *did* miss them – she missed her friends acting normal around her. Why was everything, and everyone, so weird right now?

Amy decided to focus on Josh, who was behaving the most normally out of everyone there. She copied his routine with extra care, and after a while he yelled out, 'Great stuff today, Amy! You're matching me perfectly!'

'Yeah, they have matching extra-large egos,' Asha remarked beside her, to no one in particular.

'Shut up, Asha,' Susi said.

Amy was torn between nodding gratefully at Susi and glaring at Asha, but instead of doing either, she tripped and landed in a heap on the sand.

Someone stopped the music.

'Are you OK, Amy?' Susi asked. She sounded more exasperated than sympathetic, but at least she was talking to her, unlike Asha who was making a big show of picking her nails.

At that thought, Amy's eyes filled with tears again. She absent-mindedly rubbed the ankle she'd fallen on, even though she hadn't really hurt it.

Josh was at her side in seconds. 'You look hurt! It could be a sprain.' He touched her ankle in concern and she pulled away from him quickly. She was fine and she didn't want him to touch her!

Then she remembered that Josh was partly trained in

sports medicine, that there was no way he meant anything by it and that her life was falling apart because she couldn't even react normally to having a fitness trainer touching her ankle after she'd fallen over.

'She's fine, Josh, leave her alone!' Susi hissed at the fitness trainer. 'She's just being a prima donna.'

Amy couldn't believe Susi had just said that.

Jessie came over with a clipboard and a tight-lipped expression on her face and ordered Amy to take a break. Susi let out a long, disappointed sigh and Asha tutted.

That was it. Amy looked up at Jessie. 'Actually, I'm not sure I can do any more today,' she said. 'I mean, at all. I'm sorry.'

She didn't look at anyone, and especially not Asha or Susi, as she gathered her stuff and walked off, blinking in the sunshine, to find a cab on her own.

And then, in the taxi, just when she was thinking things couldn't possibly get any worse, she went to send Damien a message and found a text on her phone from half an hour ago.

It was from *that* number.

It said: 'You bring him DOWN! He is better off without you. LEAVE HIM!'

The cab pulled up outside Rosay's villa. Rosay was expecting her, which was good because it meant Amy didn't have to worry about the guard dogs. The downside was that Rosay would only be there for about half an hour because she was about to leave for a promotional event in Italy.

After she read the message, Amy had hesitated for ages

about whether or not to confront her anonymous texter. Then she'd decided to call Rosay instead. She was sure to give Amy some good advice – about the bad publicity as well as the texts. Rosay was a proper friend. That thought made Amy think about the twins, so by the time she'd redirected the taxi at Rosay's insistence, and been met by a member of staff at Rosay's villa, her face was a mess again.

Rosay was in her dressing room doing her make-up. She turned when the maid knocked at the open door, and she greeted Amy in typical Rosay style. 'You look terrible!'

Amy rubbed her eyes. 'Thanks.'

'Don't do that! You've made it worse. Honestly, Amy!' She gestured to the array of cosmetics in front of her, which looked like an entire MAC counter at a department store, and she pulled up a velvet stool, which matched the one she was sitting on. 'Help yourself – there's a remover there and you use whatever you want to redo it. Most of this stuff's brand new.'

'No, I'm OK,' Amy sniffed, but she sat on the stool next to Rosay.

'Suit yourself.' Rosay turned away from her oversized mirror and focused on the tiny compact in her hand instead, getting to work with some false lashes. 'But you have to tell me what's going *on*? Is it about all that stuff in the papers?'

'Have you seen it?'

'Trina was on about it this morning. She loves that kind of thing – you know she's a proper gossip monger!'

'Oh. Well no, it's not that. Or not only that.'

'OK,' Rosay said, shaking out a Louis Vuitton make-up

bag full of brushes on to the dressing table and selecting a tiny lip brush. 'Spill.'

Amy started to tell Rosay about the messages; how they'd started off seeming innocent enough, but now it really seemed that someone was warning her off Damien. And possibly threatening her – she wasn't sure.

'What should I do?' she asked Rosay, who was now blotting her lips on a thin sheet of paper. 'I've got the number, but. . . I don't know.'

Rosay put down the paper and held out her hand. 'Let's see it.'

'I don't know . . .'

'Come on. Trust me. I've lived through a ton of this stuff. Remember when everyone thought I'd trashed Paige's clothes in some ridiculous revenge attack?'

'Er, yeah.' Amy couldn't forget that, really. Trina had eventually confessed to that crime, which had turned out to be a big fight over Scott White, with Trina spurred on by Claudette.

'Well, I was getting horrible anonymous messages every day back then. Honestly, Amy, I am an expert at this stuff.'

'I don't believe it,' Amy grumbled, taking her phone out of her bag. 'Really? Where do these people even get our numbers?'

'Oh, there are ways. Though often it's an inside job, if you know what I mean.'

Amy couldn't hide her shock, even though she'd kind of suspected it too, especially when she'd been standing outside Villa Dorada. It had felt as if someone knew she was there. 'Seriously? You mean, one of the others would really . . .'

'One of the others would *definitely*, Amy! Believe me, it's WAG-eat-WAG when you have a boyfriend like yours. You can't trust anyone. And it was bound to get worse now he's playing for England. There's a lot of jealousy and those girls don't half use some tricks. I'm almost glad my boyfriend's out of the spotlight.' Rosay's face went all dreamy as she waved a mascara wand around. 'Even though Scott would have loved to play for his country. It all went so wrong for him . . . Listen, you haven't told anyone about me and Scott, have you?'

Amy looked up from scrolling through messages on her phone. 'No,' she said.

'Good, because it would really be the end of me if anyone found out. You know Trina's coming with me to Milan?'

Amy shook her head.

'Yeah, she's been coming on all of my trips, like as my companion – she offered to do it when Mum couldn't, though I didn't tell her *why* Mum couldn't. And it's nice of her, and it's great to have company and all, but I might have been able to tell Mum about Scott, you know. Mum actually *likes* him, even if my step-dad doesn't.' She gave a dry laugh. 'But with Trina . . . I just have to pretend nothing's happening. I have to agree with her when she badmouths him and everything. Which happens a lot.'

'That must be hard. But what if you *did* tell her . . . I mean, she and Scott broke up a long time ago, didn't they? She'll get over it.'

Rosay shook her head firmly. 'No. There is no way in the world I'd want Trina to know. When she gets a grudge, she does not let go – ever. Besides, I only started seeing Scott as part of her grand revenge plan last year – she'll definitely think I've let her down. And you haven't seen how she gets when she's upset with someone. She's totally ruthless. You know how Claudette talked her into attacking Paige's stuff? Well, I bet she didn't take much persuading.'

Amy laughed. 'No *way* are you scared of *Trina*!'

Rosay didn't laugh. 'I'm not scared, I just . . . don't want to go there, you know? Life's stressful enough right now.' She stared into the distance, lost in her thoughts. 'Though as long as there are other big scandals taking the spotlight away from me, I'll probably be OK.' Then she shook a liquid liner as if she was shaking herself. 'Yeah, sorry, we're supposed to be talking about *you*!'

'No, it's OK, we –'

'No, come on. Trina will be here in a minute – she said she'd come and get me when it was time to go to the airstrip. So I have to shut up about Scott – and Trina – anyway! Let's see your phone, then.'

Amy handed it over with the last anonymous message displaying and she bit her lip as Rosay examined it.

'Do you think I'm overreacting?' Amy asked when Rosay was silent.

'No. No, I see what you mean. It's not nice. It'll probably get worse.'

'You think?' Amy asked miserably.

'Yeah, you want to nip that in the bud.'

'Should I text back? Or call? You know, stand up to them.'

'I don't know,' Rosay said thoughtfully. 'You probably shouldn't give whoever it is the satisfaction. Don't let them know they're getting to you.' Rosay really sounded like she was speaking from experience. 'I suppose we could withhold your number – you can do that when you call someone, but not when you text. So you could call them and hang up, see if we recognize the voice – but they still might assume it was you. No, it would be good to figure out who this is without that, and then decide what to do.'

Amy felt so relieved that she'd shared this with Rosay. She was exactly the right person after all. Asha would have rung the number instantly and given whoever answered an earful. Susi would have probably suggested telling a parent, or maybe even the police or something. But Rosay – she knew the best way to handle it.

Rosay was still staring at the phone. 'You know, the number looks familiar, but I'm not completely sure. I wish I could check, but I had all my contacts in my old phone, and that's in England.' She looked up. 'I could see if Mum's up. Or get the phone sent over by courier. Or – there's Trina. She's an absolute walking phone book – she knows everyone's number. I keep meaning to ask her to refill my contacts list.'

'I don't know . . .' Amy thought about everything Rosay had just said. 'I'm not sure about telling Trina.'

'You're not sure about telling Trina what?' said a voice from behind them.

It was Trina Santos herself, standing just outside the door with her hands on her hips and reflecting the light from the chandelier with her Stella McCartney sequinned black tank and ultra-sheer black leggings.

Rosay dropped her liquid liner with a clatter. 'How long have you been there?' she asked.

'About ten seconds, Ms Jumpy,' Trina said. 'Why? Have you been talking about me?' She laughed. 'I've had a feeling you've been hiding something from me, Rosay! So come on – tell me your secret.'

Amy tried not to look at Rosay, who was squirming quite obviously on the velvet stool. Then she decided to step in and save her friend – and anyway, what harm could it do? The more help she got with this, the better.

'It's about me. I've been getting anonymous texts,' Amy explained. 'Threatening ones, telling me to leave Damien. I wasn't sure whether to tell people or just ignore it.'

Trina's eyes widened in surprise. 'Seriously? Omigod, who from?' Then she laughed. 'Er, yeah. I'm spending so much time around Kylie, I'm turning into her. You said "anonymous", didn't you? Well, I'm glad you told me. I wonder if it's part of the anti-Amy campaign in the papers?'

'There's a *campaign*?' Amy asked. 'Against *me*?'

Trina idly tossed her hair over the racer-back of her top, like none of this was a big deal. 'Looks like it, doesn't it? All those articles appearing in a short space of time, all slating you, altering photos. You know, Amy, I think there's someone behind it. In fact, I was planning on trying to find you soon, and warning you that there was no point in talking to your PR guy about it. Because I don't think he'll help you, honey.'

'You think I shouldn't tell him?' Amy had actually forgotten she'd promised Jessie she'd speak to him. 'My producer thought I should. Why wouldn't he help me?' But she was slowly starting to realize what Trina was probably getting at.

Her PR guy, Spencer, was close friends with someone. Someone who had it in for Amy. Someone she hadn't seen for a year now, but whose last words to her had been: '*I won't forget your part in it. And yes, that's a threat . . .*' This person had said it right before making the revelation that she thought Amy had forced – a revelation that broke up her marriage to a famous footballer.

Trina was looking over Rosay's shoulder at the phone message. 'Yep. I recognize that number all right. It's not her main one – she has more than one phone so if you still have her number from before, this'll be her other one.' She looked right at Amy. 'And I don't think she was telling you to leave *Damien* alone, honey. I'm guessing she's talking about her ex-husband. She's warning you off Danny Harris. And I bet she's the one behind the media campaign too.'

'Claudette?' Amy asked, though now it was obvious.

'Claudette,' Trina confirmed with a triumphant smile.

'But she's not even here! How can she know anything about what's going on?' Though Amy could guess the answer to that one too. Claudette often got people to look out for gossip and report back to her. She could be very persuasive when she tried, and she stopped at nothing to get what she wanted. Amy herself had been roped into being one of Claudette's 'spies' in the past.

Trina looked at Amy and waited for her to answer her own question.

Amy sighed. 'Lauren,' she said. 'Lauren's been reporting everything to Claudette, hasn't she?'

Trina just smiled.

17

The next few days passed in a mass of nerves and tension between Amy and just about everyone in her life. Every time Amy's phone bleeped, her heart jumped. But so far she hadn't heard any more from the anonymous texter she now knew was Claudette. She wondered if it was a coincidence, or whether it meant Trina's plans to stop Claudette were working. Trina hadn't actually told Amy or Rosay what she was going to do; she'd just smirked and said, 'Leave it with me, girls. I'm on it. Don't mention it to Lauren either. I have a great plan!'

So whenever Amy was tempted to confront Claudette and say she knew what was going on and she wasn't going to stand for it, she reminded herself to wait for Trina to work her magic instead.

Amy also tried to keep out of Lauren's way whenever possible, and she asked the other girls to be careful what they said around her. She even mentioned it to Kylie, though Kylie didn't seem to have a clue what Amy meant and just giggled and talked about her wedding and how well Johann's team was doing.

The messages seemed to have stopped, but the media

swell against Amy hadn't. Every day there was a new negative story. They'd even dredged up some of the past and printed a photo of Amy and Josh Hunt outside a restaurant in London last summer, showing Josh kissing her innocently on the cheek. It was a photo that Rosay had said couldn't possibly be made to look bad, but the press had managed it anyway. '*What's going on HERE?*' they wrote underneath, followed by '*Taylor's girl loves playing away!*' Meanwhile football pundits and blog commenters raged and continuously blamed Amy for Damien's missed penalty. And paps regularly waited outside the hotel to leap out at Amy and follow her around, in the hope of capturing her doing something scandalous. Even worse, the inside of the Hotel Madrid was full of resident press, and even when Amy went to collect her apple in the morning, she felt like there were eyes on her, waiting for her to trip up.

She spoke to her mum and dad, but she felt really awkward then too, especially with her dad. When they asked how she was, she kept waiting for a question like, 'You're not really cheating on Damien, are you?' But they stuck to subjects like whether she was using enough sunscreen and how much paella she'd eaten, and she couldn't bring herself to blurt out, 'Mum, Dad, it's all lies!' She hoped there wasn't any trouble stirring between her parents and Damien's mum, who lived next door. Then she remembered with relief that Mrs Taylor was in London with Damien's brother right now anyway, flat-sitting and watching the World Cup on Damien's amazing plasma screen.

When it came to contacting her PR guy, Amy had ignored Jessie's advice and followed Trina's instead. She knew for a fact that he was great friends with Claudette, and she was sure that Trina was right about him not being on her side. But after a couple of days, he'd got in touch with her anyway. He sounded genuinely sorry about what was happening in the press and said he was 'doing what he could to stop it'. Amy couldn't help thinking that it obviously wasn't very much.

One thing he did do, though, was arrange for her to attend a photo shoot for the cover of *Gabriella* magazine. 'They're going for a "summer recessionista" theme, Amy. They specifically asked for you and your new budget look. They're even saying that if you can claw any of your popularity back, they could offer you a regular column. Something like "Cut-Price Glamour". Sounds right up your street, doesn't it?'

Amy agreed, and laughed about the whole idea of the shoot with Kylie and Trina the next time they all went shopping for less-than-budget clothing. Though really, Amy was starting to despair of ever seeing anything remotely nice about herself in print ever again. On the *Absolutely Amy* set, Jessie talked about 'taking each day as it comes', so every morning Amy turned up with Asha and Susi, convinced it was the day that they would all be given the boot.

Asha had apologized properly to Amy for what she said at the beach, but she still wasn't exactly being usual herself. Neither was Susi, even though she'd apologized too. In fact, everyone was acting downright weird. Asha was clearly going through the motions, barely even remembering to hurl insults at Josh any more. Susi still had that extra spring in her step that meant she'd stayed in Asha's old position for the takes and Josh constantly crowed enthusiastically about how well she was doing. But she barely spoke to Amy these days – or even Asha. And Amy ran off as fast as she could at the end of the filming every day.

Today, Amy had a good reason to beat a hasty exit. She had to be at the *Gabriella* shoot straight after *Absolutely Amy*, and after that was the third and final England game in the group round. It was the decider; after the way things had gone with the other games, and thanks to Damien's missed penalty, England now needed to beat Paraguay to get through, and if the Netherlands won their match, England could only take second place in the group.

Amy was trying to ring Damien less often so that she gave him lots of space to focus on his training, but he'd called this morning and sounded beyond nervous. She'd done her best to reassure him, all the while avoiding any mention of newspaper reports about her being 'Absolutely Amy: The Absolutely Worst Girlfriend in the World'.

The *Gabriella* shoot was at the harbour in Barcelona and none of the production team there seemed in any kind of hurry to do anything. Amy stood around as the photographer took forever to analyse the light and move his team to a slightly different location every two minutes. Then the make-up artist set up a makeshift dressing room for Amy, which basically consisted of a small screen and a folding chair in the middle of the concrete. She just about managed to hide herself from the small gathering crowd as she changed into an amazing sixties-style beaded silk-chiffon dress with a rhinestone-studded belt, which she severely doubted would fit anyone's definition of 'budget' as the label said 'One Vintage', and she knew that could be pretty exclusive stuff. Especially because she was then given a Judith Leiber clutch and silver open-toed metallic-chic Christian Louboutin shoes to match.

Then, when she perched on the folding chair to have her hair styled into intricate cascading curls, Amy wasn't hidden from anyone at all. In fact, several paps appeared and took photos of her make-up in progress.

'I cannot work with these street rats here!' the *Gabriella* photographer protested. 'If they are not removed, then I quit!'

After this, various members of staff scurried around in a panic while Amy sat on the canvas chair and worried. She was sure she was running late, but she didn't have any way of telling what the time was. Was she going to be late for the match?

An official-looking Spanish man in uniform appeared and Amy breathed a sigh of relief, hoping he'd move the paps on so that the shoot could continue. But instead he started arguing in loud Spanish with the *Gabriella* fashion director, and then he took out a notepad and started scribbling.

An assistant who'd been standing with the fashion director sauntered past. 'What's going on?' Amy asked her.

She stopped and tutted. 'It's a problem with permissions to shoot in public, or something. Apparently we've got a permit, but it's the wrong one. The paps shopped us. Ironic, huh?'

'You're kidding!' Amy bit her lip.

'Don't do that! You'll ruin your lipstick and I'll have to get make-up over again.'

Amy tried to stop. 'Do you think it'll be sorted out soon? Only –'

'Relax! Your false lashes are wobbling.' She sighed. 'Yeah, I hope it'll be soon. We have to hang on while someone calls someone who calls someone. That uniformed guy wrote it down when we didn't understand. I thought he was on about needing a "*llama*" for the shoot, which made no sense. Though we did do a shoot with an elephant once.'

'What?'

'Yeah, see what I mean? Told you it didn't make sense. But it turns out *llama* isn't one of those camel-type animals. It means "call". Listen, my Spanish isn't that good. That's all I know. Just sit there and try not to eat your make-up. I'm sure we'll get going soon enough.'

'But the game!' Amy said, panicked.

'The England game? Started ten minutes ago.' She gave her a sideways glance. 'I didn't know you were into football. Aren't you just here for the glamour and stuff?'

Amy narrowed her eyes. This had to be about a million miles away from glamorous. 'My boyfriend's on the team,' she said tightly.

'Oh, yeah, I know *that*. I just didn't think you girls actually cared about the game. Danny Harris, isn't it?' the assistant said.

'No! Damien Taylor!'

'Keep your lashes on! I can't keep up with your lot. OK, I'll send our football-crazed runner over. Don't move – those curls have to stay put.'

So Amy stayed perched on the green chair as people buzzed around her, and it seemed to take forever for a skinny

150

guy to approach her nervously and say, 'You wanted a progress report on the football? It's nearly half-time. England's winning, one–nil.'

Amy might have kissed him in gratitude if the paparazzi weren't hovering around them again. 'Who scored?'

'Harris, from a free kick thirteen minutes in.'

'Oh, brilliant!' She remembered the paps. 'I mean, brilliant that England's winning, not that Danny . . . Is Damien playing?'

'Taylor, midfielder? Yeah, he's on.' He shook his head. 'Terrible penalty the other day. Totally lost it. Nice of Vulkan to give him another chance.' He tapped his earphone. 'Half-time. We're in with a pretty good chance of getting through, but we'd be second. The Netherlands are totally trouncing Ghana.'

There was a commotion behind them.

The runner groaned. 'Oh no, looks like we're starting. I just want to listen to this!'

Amy just wanted to watch it. She considered standing up and making a break for it, like she had done at the beach the other day, but then reminded herself that she was doing this cover shoot for good publicity. Publicity that might save her image and *Absolutely Amy*, and in turn rescue things for Asha. Even though she was still vaguely annoyed with Asha, they were friends. She wanted things to work out for her.

The photography team led Amy down to the harbour, and Amy did her best to strike all the poses the photographer wanted her to, but it was hard to hide the fact that she was in a hurry to get to the game. Unfortunately, the fact that this showed on her face meant that everything took longer.

When it was finally all over she grabbed her bag and checked the time on her phone. The ninety minutes were up. She scanned the crowd of *Gabriella* staff until she found the runner with the earphone and waved to him.

He put his thumbs up and smiled. England were through.

18

'We're out. I don't believe it! We're going home.'

Amy stirred. It was Asha's voice, except that it sounded distorted and shaky. 'We're going home,' she repeated.

Amy looked around in confusion. Susi was sound asleep in the bed next to her, but Asha was fully dressed and standing at the other side of Amy's bed, holding a newspaper.

For a second, Amy wondered whether she'd dreamed the whole of yesterday afternoon. Hadn't England won? Yes, they had! She'd missed the game, but they'd definitely got through to the next round. She'd waited ages afterwards for the right time to ring Damien and congratulate him, and then when she finally had, the call had gone to voicemail. But she found out from a news report that Joe Vulkan was holding a party for the boys at Villa Dorada, so Damien was probably busy with that. Amy hoped so, anyway. Damien deserved to relax a bit. She wished she could turn up at Villa Dorada herself, like she had after the last game, but she had a feeling it wouldn't be as acceptable with the place full of team staff.

Anyway, the important thing was that England were through! They were one of the sixteen best teams in the world, and Damien played for them. It was fantastic.

And yet Asha was standing next to her bed looking like she wanted to cry.

'No, Asha, we won yesterday,' she mumbled sleepily. 'We're still in. I heard on the news that the next match is in Bilbao, and Joe Vulkan's deciding whether to move the team's base or not.'

'Oh, yeah, great. So you'll go and stay in some luxury hotel there instead, yeah? It's all right for some.'

Amy rubbed her eyes. What was Asha's problem?

'Or I suppose you could stay at this hotel and jet back and forth, and then you can hang out drinking champagne and singing karaoke all night with the WAGs, or whatever it is you lot do.' She threw the paper on the bed.

'Asha, don't start this again. You know that's not what I do. I've been home hours before you nearly every night for the past few weeks. And you haven't even really told me where you've been going, so . . .'

'I've been with Raf,' Asha stated. 'Not that I'll ever get to see him again now. Film stars don't go out of their way for nobodies.'

Amy sat up, accidentally knocking the paper on to the floor. 'Asha, what are you talking about? First of all, you're not a nobody – you're amazing! Secondly, it doesn't matter whether Raf's a film star or not. He'd be crazy not to keep seeing you, and if he doesn't, it's his loss. I can't believe I have to tell you that, when it's the kind of thing you usually tell me, and everyone else!'

Asha sniffed and sat heavily on Amy's bed, putting the paper back on her lap. 'Yeah.'

'I also can't believe you haven't told me you've been

seeing Rafael Badillo every night. I mean, I thought you'd seen him a couple of times and there was that pap photo, but . . . you didn't tell me it was *serious*!'

Asha looked guilty. 'Yeah, well, it probably isn't.' Then she looked miserable. 'For him. And I didn't tell you because I thought you'd try to talk me out of it.'

'I would have,' Amy admitted. She thought for a second. 'I still might.'

'And anyway I've been too annoyed with you lately for swanning about with your football friends, acting like a total paparazzi magnet and encouraging all the bad gossip that threatened our DVD.'

'Asha! I did *not* encourage it!' Oh my God, she sounded like Damien!

'But you didn't stop it, did you?'

'It's out of my control!' She thought of adding that Claudette was probably behind some of it, and Trina was working on putting an end to it. She could maybe even tell Asha about the horrible messages, now that they were talking properly at last.

But then Asha went all huffy again and said, 'It's not *completely* out of your control. The fact that we're going home is your fault. You didn't have to do that cover shoot yesterday.'

'I did it for *good* publicity!' Amy frowned. Asha had said it again. 'Why do you keep saying we're going home? We're not!'

'Well, you might not be, Mrs Damien Taylor. But me and Susi are.' Asha stared at the paper.

Amy wanted to lie back down and pull the duvet over

her head. 'Oh. You mean there's something bad in that paper? About me? Are you saying it's bad enough to get *Absolutely Amy* cancelled?'

Her friend nodded.

'Asha, I can't bear to look at it. Just tell me what they said.'

So Asha told Amy how she had basically let down her country by not attending her boyfriend's match, but preferring to sit on a chair by the harbour having her hair and make-up done for some shallow cover picture. The headline read: '*ShAMY on you!*' and underneath it said: '*WAG chooses glamour over support for country!*' and the picture was of Amy surrounded by *Gabriella* staff fussing over a single curl as Amy cast a bored look at her sparkly Louboutin shoes. The *Daily News* 'Girl Talk' columnist was very glad that the boys had got through, but it was '*England 1, Amy Thornton 0*'.

Jessie's call came through a couple of minutes after Asha finished her summary. It woke up Susi and it confirmed Asha's fears. The powers had spoken. Amy Thornton was hated by English women everywhere and Jessie's boss thought the DVD was not going to sell. The production was over. Jessie was sorry – really sorry, they had no idea. 'The hotel's paid up till the end of the week and we'll be in touch with a voucher for the return flight,' she said just before she hung up. 'Good luck, girls, and thanks. At least we had a good run with the first DVD.'

Susi groaned, turned over and went back to sleep. Asha said she was going for a walk and slammed the door behind her.

Amy sat back and wondered how she could have messed up so badly. The *Gabriella* shoot had been arranged to rescue her image, not make things even worse! She should ring her PR guy and tell him how things had backfired. Maybe he could still work out a way to rescue her, and this whole situation. If only yesterday's shoot hadn't been so public! Those paps had gathered almost immediately. And then they'd even caused a delay by raising issues about *Gabriella*'s permit. It was as if . . . as if they'd done it on purpose.

And maybe they had, Amy realized. Maybe someone had told them to do it.

Claudette had a hotline to the paparazzi. Last summer, Claudette had often arranged for publicity, especially when she was doing something glamorous and pap-worthy. What if she'd called them and told them to attend the *Gabriella* shoot? Or what if Spencer the PR guy had done it? Maybe they'd even asked the paps to delay the proceedings. Maybe it was all deliberate.

Amy knew she couldn't call Spencer. She couldn't trust him.

She was so resigned to everything going wrong for her that she almost didn't flinch when she checked her phone and there was a message from *that* number. It read: 'England are through, but you are OUT!'

Amy got dressed and headed for the roof terrace bar so that she could make a phone call without disturbing Susi.

It was time to talk to Trina again.

Trina proved to be hard to track down. Amy didn't have her number so she rang Rosay first, thinking they might be together anyway, at some exotic singing engagement. But Rosay was having a rare day at the villa with her step-dad, and she reported that Trina and Kylie were out with their boyfriends, as far as she knew.

'How are things going?' Amy asked her. 'How's your mum? And are you going to the greenhouse later, if Trina's out?'

Rosay laughed and said her mum was a tiny bit better, though still refusing to leave the house back in London. 'And I don't meet Scott in the greenhouse any more,' she said. 'Not since I was found out!' She laughed. 'He's got one of those luxury apartments – you know, near Café Biarritz? It's pretty exclusive around there. Everyone's so self-absorbed and rich that I reckon I can get away with sneaking in and out sometimes!'

They talked about what had happened with *Absolutely Amy* and Rosay instantly offered rooms at the villa to Amy, Asha and Susi. She said her step-dad wouldn't mind, and possibly wouldn't even notice, that's how distracted he'd been since his wife got ill.

'Wow, no, we couldn't,' Amy said. She was supposed to be supporting herself – or at least having her work pay for expenses. But it was so tempting. She didn't want to miss any more of Damien's matches, and watching them on telly wouldn't be the same. 'Anyway, it would take a miracle to persuade Asha and Susi's mum to accept something like that.'

'Aw, that's a shame. But you can stay by yourself, can't you? Well, with Trina and Kylie in the guest wing.'

Amy said she'd think about it. Anyway, it might take some

work to persuade *her* parents, too. When she said bye to Rosay, she sent her mum and dad a message saying she'd speak to them very soon. She needed to figure things out a bit more first.

She called Trina on the number she'd got from Rosay, but there was no reply. The voicemail recording must have been recently changed because it said: 'Trina's out celebrating! Leave a message!'

Amy wondered if Trina was still partying from last night. She thought about turning up at Rio Grande, which was probably open and full of last night's revellers. But it would just seem weird turning up somewhere like that in the cold light of morning. She sent Trina a quick message instead: 'Hope ur OK? Got another of those txts :('

She tried Damien one more time, but he still wasn't answering his phone. Maybe he was still partying too. She wished she could be with him – after all, it was another 'family day' – but she put that thought out of her head and headed back to the hotel room. The sun beamed through the window and Amy thought it was the perfect day for a long swim in the sea instead of a ten-minute struggle to complete a lap in the Hotel Madrid's mermaid pool. She decided she'd find a nice beach and have the best day ever, even if it had to be all by herself.

When she was ready, Amy left a sleeping Susi in the hotel room and went downstairs to ask the hotel receptionist for advice about the most fabulous beach she could reach quickly by taxi. She tried to keep her voice low so that the journalist guests around didn't hear, but the receptionist replied loudly, 'There's a very exclusive beach resort nearby,

Miss Thornton. Only celebrity guests are allowed, and usually no press. I'm sure they will welcome you. You are very famous right now.'

A man who'd been leafing through the paper at the other end of the reception desk snorted and said, 'Infamous, more like.'

Some other people stopped and stared at Amy, and their expressions weren't friendly. Amy tried to ignore them as she waited for the receptionist to call a taxi and give instructions to the driver.

She nearly laughed when, half an hour later, the taxi pulled up at a place she recognized. It was Las Playas resort, the location of the party she'd been at right at the beginning of her stay in Spain. And the receptionist was right that she was waved in and welcomed like a VIP, but Amy was suddenly hit by a wave of sadness when she realized that she'd increased her celebrity status since her arrival, but for all the wrong reasons. The DVD had been called off and she wasn't even working any more – she was just known for being someone who had a footballer boyfriend. Or possibly two. And she was letting one, or possibly both, of them down regularly and publicly. It wasn't the way she'd planned on spending her summer, that was for sure. Not to mention the fact that she was going to have to explain all this to her mum and dad – if they hadn't already read a version of it in the paper. And why hadn't Damien called her back? She knew he'd had that party last night, but surely he'd be up by now? He had his training, didn't he? But she'd left him a few messages now and she was starting to think he didn't want to speak to her.

She'd just decided to stop checking her phone and head to the sea when a message came through. Her heart leapt, but it was from Trina: 'Am working on it RIGHT NOW. C will be sorry! T x'

Amy sighed and sent Trina a quick thank-you text. Then she put her phone away, dumped her bag and headed for the water, trying to put her worries out of her mind as she whipped strongly through the waves. She swam and swam, away from the wide beach and towards a cluster of moored speedboats, then round a craggy rock, heading for a pebbly beach that looked even more exclusive than Playa Menor. As she neared the shore, and just when she thought that her beautiful surroundings were finally cheering her up, she heard it. Helicopters overhead. Paparazzi – just like the other time she'd been at Playa Menor.

They couldn't possibly be here for her this time, could they? She felt like ducking under the water and doing some deep-sea diving until they'd gone.

But maybe it was time to face them, anyway. She shouldn't be hiding – it would probably only make everything worse. Maybe she'd find a reporter and tell them her side of the story. She could even show them what Claudette was doing. She had the messages on her phone – she had evidence!

The water became too shallow for swimming and she stood, adjusting her bikini before she remembered that the paps might take a picture of her doing it, ringed and labelled something like: '*Amy's wardrobe malfunction!*'.

But the buzzing didn't move any closer and she wondered whether there might be someone more gossip-worthy on the tiny beach.

Amy pulled herself on to a nearby flat rock. She sat back so that she could get a good look at the beach while still being hidden from view.

She recognized him straight away. It was the captain of the England team, shirtless and completely fit-looking.

And the only other person on the beach was Trina herself.

Danny Harris and Trina Santos were on a private beach together. They were pretty far apart – Danny was at the water's edge skimming stones and Trina was standing further back, shielding her eyes from the sun as she pressed buttons on her phone. But Amy was sure the paps would still make something of it. This would be all over the gossip magazines by the end of the week.

Amy couldn't believe she hadn't realized it before. Trina's boyfriend, Nik, was on a team that had been eliminated in the first round. Ghana were going home. So when Trina had said she was 'celebrating', she can't have meant she was with Nik Sika. She must have meant she was celebrating England's success . . . with Danny Harris.

Amy remembered a conversation she'd had with Trina ages ago where Trina made it clear she fancied Danny. And then she remembered Rosay telling her that Trina could be ruthless. But she couldn't believe Trina had really swapped men so easily! What were they doing here on the beach together?

The helicopters got closer and Trina tossed her mane of hair over one shoulder, clearly posing. She called over to Danny and he turned towards her, throwing a pebble in the air and chipping it expertly with his foot. The cameras swooped.

Amy thought about the text Trina had sent her not very long ago, and she wondered whether this was all part of Trina's plan. Maybe Trina was doing this for her – the press would stop spreading rumours about her and Danny if they saw him with Trina. Plus there was no surer way of getting at Claudette Harris than being linked to her ex-husband, as Amy already knew to her cost. Amy could just imagine Trina sending gloating texts to Claudette about this.

But what about Danny? Did he know he was stuck in the middle of some game? A game Trina was probably playing for Amy's sake?

Amy felt uncomfortable, and it wasn't just because the rock was uneven and sharp on the backs of her legs. She wasn't sure whether to be pleased that Trina's plan was clearly in motion, or worried and slightly guilty. She was definitely relieved that the paps were paying absolutely zero attention to her for a change, though.

When the helicopters buzzed away and the beach returned to its former tranquillity, Amy considered going over to say hi to Trina and Danny. But Danny said something to Trina and they quickly gathered their things and made their way to a speedboat, which was moored nearby, by another set of rocks. Amy noticed there was someone waiting in the boat – obviously the skipper. He helped Trina and Danny on board and the three of them sped away, leaving a trail of swirling white foam in their wake.

19

The days that followed were a bit of a nightmare. Amy spent so much time sitting in the hotel room that she thought she may as well just go home and give up on her supposedly fun summer in Spain anyway. It was certainly turning out to be anything but.

She was so determined to prove to Asha and Susi that she wasn't expecting any special treatment that she made a great show of not contacting Rosay, Kylie or Trina or spending any time with them. They were all pretty busy now anyway – Kylie was putting the finishing touches on her wedding arrangements, Rosay was making local singing appearances and Trina was firmly in the public eye after the Danny gossip got out, even though apparently Danny had 'denied having any kind of relationship with Trina Santos'. Amy figured she'd find out soon enough exactly what Trina was up to. She still felt a mixture of gratitude and worry when she thought about it. The text messages from Claudette had stopped, and Amy really hoped Trina wasn't getting them instead.

In the meantime, she made a huge effort with Asha and Susi, hoping to make the most of their last few days before they had to give up the hotel room. She suggested low-budget things they could do, like shopping in the local markets or even just sitting on the beach. But Asha seemed determined to mope in the hotel room, saying this was probably the last time in her life she'd ever be in a hotel room like this and she wanted to savour it. She'd already told Raf that it was over between them because it could never work.

'How did he take it?' Amy asked when Asha told her about that, two days after the cancellation of *Absolutely Amy*.

Asha flicked the television on to watch an old episode of *Friends* dubbed into Spanish. 'He pretended to be upset,' she said dully. 'I wasn't fooled.'

'Oh, Asha, *course* he was upset!'

Amy turned to Susi for support, but Susi was utterly useless these days. She was bouncing distractedly around again. Then she said she had to be somewhere and she bounded out of the room altogether.

'Don't you ever wonder where she's going?' Amy asked Asha.

Asha shushed her until the adverts came on and then said, 'Not really. She's Susi. She'll be fine. She probably spends her days shopping for bargain presents for our little cousins. And the evenings at under-18s salsa classes, knowing her.'

'But have you noticed how, you know, bouncy and happy she's seemed lately?'

'It's probably because she doesn't have to cover for me and Raf any more,' Asha pouted.

Amy's love life wasn't much better than Asha's. She'd finally managed to get hold of Damien, but he'd been really frosty with her on the phone. She'd tried so hard not to have an argument with him as she told him about what had happened to *Absolutely Amy* and he hadn't really seemed very sympathetic.

'I can see their point,' he'd said. 'I mean, publicity like that reflects badly on them.'

Amy wanted to ask whether he also thought it reflected badly on *him*, but she was too scared of the answer. So instead she told him about seeing Trina with Danny, thinking he might be pleased that Steve could stop that particular line of taunting.

But Damien just said, 'She's trouble.'

'Joe Vulkan would say *all* girls are trouble. They all get in the way of football,' she tried to joke.

Damien didn't laugh. 'So if the DVD thing's over, are you off home?' he asked, and her heart nearly broke at how off-hand he sounded.

She thought she'd better face it head-on. 'Damien, are you annoyed with me for not being at your match? Because you know, it was completely unavoidable.'

'No, yeah, it's fine. You shouldn't have to interrupt your important photo shoots to watch me play football.' He paused, then he added, 'For England.'

'OK, stop it.'

'What?'

'*You* know,' Amy sighed, exasperated. 'Stop believing what the press say about me. OK, so they think I'm not supporting you, but you don't think that.' She hesitated. 'Do you?'

The silence after that went on forever. Too long. Amy's heart sank more with every passing millisecond.

'Sorry, Ames,' Damien said eventually. 'It's been difficult, you know.'

'I know. For me too.'

'Yeah, sure.'

'It *has*!'

'I know! I said "sure". I miss you, Ames.'

She sighed. 'OK, so is there any chance of seeing you after your next match? Because that's the day before we're supposed to leave the hotel and, you know . . .' Amy took a deep breath. 'Go back to England.' She hadn't really decided what to do about Rosay's offer of a place to stay for the rest of the tournament, and she hadn't done anything about booking a flight home with her *Absolutely Amy* flight voucher, either. Her mum had said it was up to Amy. Her dad had said she should come home and stay out of trouble, but he'd understand if she wanted to stay and he didn't trust a word he read in the newspapers any more. She was glad they were taking it so well, but it didn't help with her decision. She couldn't mention it to Asha or Susi because *their* mum had already made them book a flight for the day the hotel booking ran out, and she knew there was no way they'd be allowed to stay a minute longer.

Amy hadn't realized it until this second, but she was actually waiting for Damien to help her decide.

Or at least to sound like he cared either way.

'Amy, you know I don't take time off,' he said. 'I've told you a hundred times. Don't make me feel bad about it.'

She couldn't believe he'd said that! She took a deep breath. 'No, OK, I won't. I understand.'

'Thanks, I –'

'Yeah, I understand completely. It would be easier for you if I wasn't here, wouldn't it? Or maybe even if . . .' She thought about the last anonymous message she'd got, the one that said she brought him down, and she should leave him. Trina said it was about Danny, but it certainly seemed to apply to her and Damien. Wasn't that exactly what the papers were saying? That she was ruining Damien's – and England's – chances? Would it be better if Damien didn't have to worry about her at all? If their relationship finished . . . Damien wouldn't have any threat of distraction. And then the paps would have to leave her alone.

'If *what*?' Damien asked sharply.

He hadn't questioned the first part of what she said. He hadn't insisted he wanted her here.

'If . . .' But she couldn't bring herself to say it. 'Never mind.' Suddenly she didn't want to talk to him any more at all. 'Listen, I've got to go. Bye, Damien.'

'Amy . . .'

'I'll see you some time, OK?'

She hung up, wondering why it felt like she'd said 'see you *around*'. Like she actually had finished with him.

This was Damien. They'd been together for three years! They couldn't split up over this. Turned out this long-distance relationship thing really was tough. Especially when your boyfriend was actually just up the road from you, but he refused to see you, even when he was allowed.

Since then, they'd texted each other, but not really said anything important or even anything that proved they weren't on the brink of breaking up. It made Amy want to cry whenever she thought about it, but she didn't know how to sort things out.

'Don't give up on him, Amy,' Rosay said to her when Amy phoned her for a long chat about the whole situation. Rosay was in a very obvious loved-up state over Scott, and she thought everyone should be like her. 'Ballers go crazy during important tournaments and it doesn't mean he doesn't want to be with you.'

'I don't know,' Amy sniffed.

'I do. It seems like the world's against you right now, but it won't last forever.' Rosay's voice was bouncy as she added, 'Tell you what! You should definitely stay at the villa for as long as you want and show those tabloids – and Damien – how supportive you really are. You can even use my step-dad's private plane to go to Bilbao for the next match. OK?'

'Well, OK,' Amy agreed. 'Thanks, Rosay.'

After that, she stressed non-stop about admitting to Asha and Susi that she was staying, especially after everything Asha had accused her of, so she stalled for time whenever they asked what she was doing. She put it off for so long that by the day before they had to check out of Hotel Madrid, which was also the day of England's first knock-out match, Amy still hadn't told them.

And then she finally told Asha, but there were other things to worry about.

Because Amy and Asha woke up that Saturday morning and Susi wasn't there.

20

At first, they hadn't worried.

No, it was worse than that. At first, they hadn't even noticed she'd gone.

Amy, who was already feeling slightly nostalgic for the tiny mermaid pool even though she was headed for the luxury of Rosay's huge outdoor pool, had decided to creep out of the room early, before it was even light, for a short, cramped swim. As she got out of bed, Asha stirred and mumbled something about wanting to go for her 'last ever hotel breakfast', because tomorrow, check-out day, would be too much of a rush. Still half asleep, they'd both got dressed quickly in the semi-dark so as not to wake up Susi because Susi never had breakfast anyway. After her swim, Amy went straight to the breakfast room to see Asha, and they joked about having left Susi sleeping upstairs.

'Her salsa classes must be pretty exhausting,' Asha commented. 'Maybe when your hips don't lie, you need to sleep it off for ages afterwards.'

Amy laughed. Then she finally admitted to Asha that she was staying in Spain, at least for now.

'Oh, that's a surprise,' Asha said sarcastically, but with a smile. 'Well, lucky you. Tell me all about it when you're back in Stanleydale. Though don't tell me if you see Raf with anyone else at any glam parties. Or anywhere. I don't want to know.'

'Ash, I still don't understand why you broke up with him,' Amy said. 'He lives in Spain, not the other side of the world. Why couldn't you still see each other?'

'He lives in southern California, Amy. And he works on films all over the world, but never in Stanleydale.' She gave a wry smile. 'He's only here for the football, and to visit his family in Northern Spain for a bit. After that, I'd never see him.'

'I don't see Damien all that much,' Amy said. Not that it wasn't causing problems between them.

'Yeah, well, it's not for me. I'm not hanging about pathetically waiting for crumbs of his time as he lives his film-star life, meeting all those gorgeous actresses and models and . . . you know.' She nudged Amy. 'Footballers' girlfriends.' She stood up. 'Come on. We'd better wake my sister up. Me and Susi have got packing and present-buying to do today. And you have to be at some champagne cocktail lunch with your rich friends, probably.'

'Close. I have to take a private jet to a World Cup game in Bilbao.' Amy smiled, relieved that Asha seemed OK about it after all.

They deliberately clattered back into the hotel room, trying to wake Susi. Then Asha ripped the curtains open as noisily as she could. And that's when they noticed that Susi's bed was neatly made, complete with that hotel-look folded down corner.

'Did she get up while we were downstairs?' Amy wondered out loud.

'I don't think so. Susi's sensible and all, but I've never seen her make a bed like that, ever. You know we're more a shake-your-duvet-and-go kind of family.'

'Well, maybe she's still out? From last night?'

'At the salsa class?' Asha asked, but her voice didn't sound jokey any more. She sat down heavily on Susi's bed. 'Omigod, Amy. She didn't come back last night, did she? Do you . . .' Her voice trembled. 'Do you think something's happened to her?'

'No, Ash, wait –'

'Omigod, omigod, I don't even know where she might have gone! I've been so wrapped up in myself, and all this Raf stuff! It's all I've talked to her about, too, you know. And then I've been accusing *you* of being selfish –'

'You haven't!'

'I have. But I'm a million times worse! She's my *sister*, Amy! My twin sister, and I don't even know where she was last night! Or the night before! Or . . .' Asha let out a single sob.

Amy rushed over to put her arm round Asha. 'Calm down, Ash. It's OK. It's OK.'

'*How* is it OK? Where's Susi?'

'We'll call her,' Amy said, trying to keep her voice as steady as she could. 'Maybe she's at one of those twenty-four-hour clubs.'

'*Susi?* Without us?'

'You said yourself we've been far too wrapped up in ourselves,' Amy said, picking up her phone. 'Maybe we've missed something. Have a quick look around. See if there are any clues about where she could be.'

'Like what?' Asha moved towards Susi's bed, her eyes staring and panicky. 'Tell me what to look for, Amy!'

'I don't know.' Amy felt out of her depth, but someone had to be the calm one. Though of the three of them, that was usually Susi's job. Amy's heart sank. She thought about detective films she'd seen. 'Like . . . a book of matches in the pocket of her jeans or . . .'

'Susi doesn't smoke!'

'I know, I know.' Amy tried Susi's number, but only reached a message saying the phone was switched off. 'Look, I'm trying, Ash, but I –'

Asha interrupted her with a yelp. 'Her stuff's gone!' She frantically opened and closed drawers and cupboards. 'Her best jeans have gone! Her make-up bag is gone! Susi's gone! Omigod, omigod!'

'Ash, Ash, calm down. It's a good sign!'

'Why?' Asha's eyes pleaded with her, as if Amy could solve everything and make Susi reappear with just words.

'Because . . .'

Asha stared at her.

'Because it means she *wanted* to go. She planned it. So probably nothing bad's happened to her.'

'Probably?' Asha yelped.

Amy spoke slowly and steadily. 'No, look. It's the day before your flight, and she's taken her important stuff. She's switched her phone off.' She took a deep breath. 'She's . . . she's run away, Asha.'

Asha stared at her. 'Omigod. *Susi*'s run away?'

'Yeah, it looks like it. To avoid going home, maybe. Don't you think?'

'It's what *she'd* think if it was the other way round,' Asha said.

'What do you mean?'

Asha blinked back tears. 'I was talking to her all last week about it. About how I was going to run away if I was forced to go back to Stanleydale. I said I'd pack my bags in the night and sneak off and not tell anyone where I was going. But I didn't really mean it.'

'And what did she say?'

'She said . . .' Asha thought for a while. 'She said it sounded tempting.'

'That doesn't sound like her,' Amy said.

'You're right. You're right, it really doesn't. And I was too busy thinking about Raf to notice!'

Amy took charge after that. She tried to think of everyone who knew Susi and whose numbers they had – except parents, after Asha begged her not to call them, not yet. Unfortunately, it boiled down to three people. Jessie the producer, Josh and Rosay.

She tried Jessie first, but got a hurried reply on a very bad connection. 'Sorry, Amy, I can't talk. We're boarding right now!'

'You're leaving today?'

'Yes, most of the team is. They're all here with me.' The next part of what Jessie said disappeared into a warped static noise.

'Listen, sorry to bother you,' Amy said quickly. 'Have you seen Susi?'

'Pardon? Susi? No, she's about the only one who's not

here, apart from you and Asha.' Another burst of static engulfed Jessie's words. 'Sorry, Amy, I can't hear a thing and I have to switch my phone off – I'll call later from England, OK?'

There didn't seem to be much point in calling Josh after that, but Amy tried it anyway, and sure enough there was no reply. He was obviously on the plane with Jessie. Amy told Asha she'd try them both again in a few hours.

Asha paced around the hotel room as Amy tried the final call. Rosay answered immediately and her voice was weird. Amy forgot her own troubles for a split second. 'Are you OK? Is your mum OK?'

'Oh. Yeah,' Rosay replied in a strained voice.

'Never mind her mum! Ask about Susi,' Asha mumbled in the background, thankfully pretty quietly.

'Who's that? Omigod, you haven't been telling people about Mum, have you?' Rosay's voice was full of accusation.

'No, of course not!'

Rosay seemed to relax a bit. 'OK. OK. Sorry, I'm just . . . nervous. I'm about to go to a promotional thing in Bilbao with Trina. So what's up?'

Amy told her about Susi, and Rosay said she didn't know anything, but she'd help in any way she could.

After she hung up, Amy thought about texting Damien, but she couldn't worry him before his match, and anyway she didn't think he'd be able to help. She just wanted to talk to him because he knew the twins almost as well as she did and . . . Or maybe she just wanted to talk to him. Then she felt irrationally annoyed with him for being completely unreachable when she needed him.

Amy and Asha packed their stuff in silence, partly to be ready for checking out of the hotel tomorrow, but mostly just for something to do while they decided on their next move. Every now and then, Amy stopped to call Susi, but her phone was still switched off. Then Asha would say, 'I never thought she could do anything like this,' and Amy had to agree with her. She really wished she could say something to Asha to stop her worrying, but the truth was she was pretty worried herself. She thought about all the times recently that she and Asha had more or less told Susi she was boring and safe. Amy realized that Susi had been getting increasingly annoyed with them about that. Even so, Amy couldn't believe she could just take off like this.

They pushed their cases to one side and went to catch the bus into the city centre, where Asha had some ideas of places they could search.

'Places I went to with Raf,' she admitted. 'And Susi came along sometimes, when she wasn't staying in at the hotel to ring Mum and pretend I was asleep and stuff, to cover for me . . .' She stopped. 'Oh. She probably wasn't at the hotel, was she?'

'She was never there when I got back early, which was a lot.' Amy had never considered before that the twins might not have been together on those nights.

'D'you think she called Mum from somewhere else? It had to be somewhere quiet, though – I couldn't ring myself because I was in clubs and stuff.'

'I don't know. I always thought she was with you.'

'You were always both sleeping when *I* got in,' Asha said. 'But don't tell Mum I was out so late with . . . Omigod, we're going to *have* to tell Mum! And soon. I can't get on that plane tomorrow without her.'

Amy hugged her friend. 'We'll find her. Look, I'll try to reach Jessie and Josh again in a bit. They have to land eventually. You keep trying Susi.'

'We've already tried her phone a hundred times.'

'Yeah, true. OK, well, there must be someone else who knows something. What about . . . What about boys?'

'You think she has a secret boyfriend? Oh God, not Susi! No way!'

'No, course not. I meant the boys in our lives. Damien knows Susi, but I can't call him now. And anyway, he's been training non-stop – he wouldn't know a thing. But no, I meant, what about Rafael? He's met Susi lots of times, hasn't he? He might have seen something we haven't, or know somewhere she'd go.'

'I'm not ringing him, Amy,' Asha said dramatically.

'Asha,' Amy said. 'For Susi?'

Asha stared at her phone. 'I can't. I told him I'd never speak to him again.'

'Why? I thought you just told him things wouldn't work out.'

'Well, yeah, but I laid it on a bit thick. I had to, otherwise I'd have changed my mind.'

'Oh, Asha, honestly!'

Asha shrugged and they both fell into a worried silence as they walked along the wide pavements.

'There's a place just up here we should try,' Asha said at last. 'A cafe I often went to in the afternoons with Raf, and Susi came with us a few times. When she wasn't going home for a nap.' She sighed. '*Supposedly* going home for a nap. Anyway, she said she liked the place.'

'OK, let's go.'

'It's just round this corner. Café Biarritz. Raf absolutely loves it there. It's full of his kind of people – people with money to burn on overpriced drinks.'

'Oh, Café Biarritz? I've been there!'

'With your "friends"?'

'Um, yeah.'

Asha squinted into the distance as they neared the large building. 'Looks like one of them is there right now.'

Amy glanced over. 'Who?'

It was Lauren. She was sitting on her own at an outside table, dressed in a trying-too-hard blue silk-look jumpsuit. She was busy texting – probably telling Claudette all the latest scandals, knowing her.

'She's not a friend. She's the biggest gossip in the world,' Amy said. 'Have you forgotten what a stirrer she was last summer?'

'I remember.' Asha shuddered. 'I don't like her either – she's always in here when I come in with Raf, asking tons of questions. I can't help thinking she's snooping around.'

Amy could imagine. 'Yeah, she probably is. I'll tell you all about it some time.'

'But if she's such a gossip, she might know something about Susi.'

Amy thought about Claudette, waiting at home for reports. 'No, I think she's only after WAG stuff. Besides, I don't want to speak to her,' she said, just as Lauren looked up, saw Amy and waved excitedly. As if she hadn't just been sat there texting poisonous gossip that could ruin people's lives. Including Amy's.

Asha gave her a tiny shove in the direction of the cafe. 'Amy. For Susi,' she said.

Amy groaned and walked over, with Asha right behind her. 'There's no way she can help us,' Amy grumbled quietly on the way.

The first thing Lauren said was, 'Hi, Amy. And . . . Asha, isn't it? Haven't seen you for a few days. Raf's been in, though, acting all cut up about you dumping him.'

'Oh,' Asha mumbled under her breath.

'Don't worry, I'm right with you. I dumped Steve recently too. A girl's got to have her pride, don't you think?' She looked like she didn't quite believe it. 'I found out he two-timed me with Courtney and . . . well, never mind. It's over now.' She took a sip of her mineral water. 'But I miss him! Do you think I should turn up to the game? Maybe he'll see me on the family day . . .'

Asha shifted impatiently. Amy wanted to say 'I told you she'd be useless' but it seemed a bit mean now that Lauren was heartbroken. She thought it, though.

'Steve's just confused, I think. He's not like some of those footballers, out for whatever they can get.' Lauren leant towards Asha and Amy like she had a huge secret. 'You'll never guess who I saw coming out of those apartments across from here the other day?'

Amy didn't want to guess. She remembered Rosay telling her that Scott lived in those apartments.

'Only Rosay Sands, that's who! And I've heard Scott

White has a place there. Do you reckon she's seeing him again? I do!'

'I'm sure it wasn't her,' Amy said quickly. 'Or I'm sure it's not what you're thinking.' She thought she'd better warn Rosay as soon as possible that Lauren might be on to her.

'If you say so,' Lauren smirked. 'But . . . Scott White? There's the kind of footballer no girl should be involved with. Not like Steve, who just hasn't worked out what's good for him yet.' She turned to Asha. 'What about you and your film star? You think you'll ever forgive Raf for whatever he did?'

Asha frowned. 'It wasn't like that. He wasn't seeing anyone else.'

'Oh, right.' Lauren laughed. 'You know, I thought I saw you here yesterday, shamelessly flaunting some new man in front of Raf already, but it turned out to be your twin sister! Susi, right? With that super-fit fitness instructor?'

Amy and Asha looked at each other and then at her.

Lauren continued chattily, 'Ooh, aren't they off on that boat trip now? They were asking Raf about it yesterday. You know, what with his brother having that boat-chartering business in San Sebastian, or whatever he was on about. They were dead keen – said they wanted to leave right away. Josh was on about swimming in the proper ocean, or something.'

Asha gasped. 'What are you talking about?'

'Josh is on a plane to England,' Amy said doubtfully.

'No, he's definitely on some kind of mini-break thing with Susi. I heard all about their plans,' Lauren said matter-of-factly. 'You know, until yesterday, I didn't even realize they were an item. You never tell me anything, Amy!'

Amy gripped the table as Asha blurted loudly, 'No way!'

'Seriously, she didn't tell me!' Lauren said, missing the point. 'Hey, want me to spread the word about this online, Amy? We should have thought of it before! If it gets out then people might finally stop gossiping about you and Josh, eh?' She frowned. 'What? Why are you both looking at me like you're dying of shock?'

21

Amy stared out of the window at the dusty-looking deserted road, heat shimmering on tarmac as the taxi made its way along the coast of northern Spain.

If Amy wanted to be the supportive, perfect girlfriend – the one she needed to be to get back in favour with the tabloids, and possibly to save her relationship with Damien – then she was in completely the wrong place. She should have been further west, in the city where Damien would soon be playing in England's first knockout match of the tournament, the city Rosay's private plane was supposed to have landed in.

Instead they had re-routed to the resort of San Sebastian, where Rafael Badillo's family lived, and where Raf was right now waiting for them.

Amy had phoned Raf after Lauren's revelation about Susi and Josh. Or rather, after she'd talked Asha into letting her.

'She's talking rubbish!' Asha said at first, after they'd left Lauren in Café Biarritz, sipping her water, texting and clearly listening out for more gossip. Amy couldn't help wondering whether she was still going to be any use to Claudette now that she wasn't officially a WAG any more, but maybe she would. Lauren certainly seemed to have supreme gossip-gathering skills.

'Now I see what you mean about that girl,' Asha said as they walked past the gated apartments where Scott White was staying. 'She thinks she knows everything about everyone, but she doesn't really know a thing. You said Josh was with Jessie on that plane to England.'

'I thought so. But the connection was so bad, I didn't exactly hear every word Jessie said.'

And sure enough, a few minutes later, Jessie had phoned from England and confirmed that Josh wasn't with her – something she apparently had told Amy before, but it must have been swallowed by static. Jessie didn't know where Susi or Josh were but she didn't seem remotely surprised by the idea that they might have gone somewhere together.

Even after that call, Asha said, 'They're all wrong. There's just no way my sister is seeing Josh!'

'I don't know . . .' Amy could sort of picture it. The night of the opening ceremony, hadn't she left Susi to talk to Josh? And Susi hadn't seemed to mind. Then later, when Amy had called, Susi had been extra-giggly and happy. Amy wondered whether that was where it had all started, and it did make sense. She thought about the way Susi and Josh were always off in corners talking quietly on the *Absolutely Amy* set. And who knew how much they met up away from the shoots? She and Asha had already established that they didn't have a clue where Susi had been going, or who with.

Asha gave Amy a horrified look. 'Oh no! Even *you* think it's true? Right. That does it.' She took her phone out and pressed a button. 'Susi's still not answering. Fine. I'm ringing

Josh.' But when he didn't answer either, Asha panicked. 'I need to speak to Susi now! I need to tell her to break up with him right this second!'

'See, Asha, maybe this is why she kept it secret from you,' Amy said.

Asha glared at her. 'OK, smug-face, so why did she keep it a secret from *you*?'

'Because . . .' Amy bit her lip guiltily. 'Maybe because everyone thought Josh fancied me. I mean, it was in all the papers . . .'

'Wait – you mean *you* thought Josh still fancied you, don't you?'

Amy shrugged.

'Oh well, I don't blame Susi for not telling *you* then! I bet that was really annoying for her, having you thinking you were Josh's first choice and she was second best. I remember that feeling.'

'*You're* the one who thought he asked me out to Rosay's party!' Amy thought about it. 'Oh wow – when Josh invited me, he kept asking whether "the twins" would come. He meant Susi, didn't he?'

Asha shuddered. 'I'm glad he didn't mean *me*. Honestly, I could kill him.'

'At least we know Susi's safe.'

Asha shook her head. 'No, we don't! Look at the way he's made her take off like this, making us worry ourselves sick – he's practically kidnapped her!'

'Hang on, Asha. Do you really think Josh is that bad?'

'I don't know,' Asha said sulkily. 'Maybe not.'

'Because we don't know that Josh *made* her leave. It might

have been her decision. She might not even have told him we don't know about it. And not being able to reach them by phone – that could be because there's no reception at sea, couldn't it?'

'I don't know. I need to see her – I need to be sure she's OK! Anyway, what does Josh know about boats? I know Susi doesn't know anything. And she's not exactly a strong swimmer, is she?'

Amy and Asha had both been lifeguards at the local water park back home, but Susi had worked in the cafe.

'Besides, we need to go home tomorrow! No, I have to see her! I have to talk to her. But how am I going to find her when all we have to go on is the fact that Josh talked to Raf about hiring a boat from some cousin of his?'

Amy looked at her.

'Oh, no. No, no, I'm not ringing Raf.'

'Then I will.'

'Amy, don't you have to leave for that match in about five minutes?'

'No, I have to help my friends, right now. Give me your phone. Please?'

Amy had to cajole Asha for about ten minutes before she finally handed her phone over. First Amy spoke to Raf and then she rang Rosay and explained as much as she could, since Rosay and Trina were now late for their event. Rosay sounded super-rushed and still a bit weird, but she insisted that it was fine for the plane to be re-routed to San Sebastian, and she asked a few concerned questions about where Raf was meeting them and where they were likely to go.

Amy hung up before she realized she'd forgotten to warn

Rosay about Lauren. She'd tell her next time. Rosay was in a hurry and it could wait.

Before long Amy and Asha were on their way to San Sebastian in Carlo di Rossi's private plane.

The taxi slowed down and snaked its way through the old town. San Sebastian was gorgeous. They travelled through a maze of narrow streets, markets and bustle, with colourful washing hanging on the small balconies of sun-soaked buildings at every turn.

They pulled up at the harbour, a tidy rectangle of moored boats nestled beneath mossy green and brown mountains. The water looked darker and greyer than the sea Amy had got used to off the coast near Barcelona, but it was just as inviting.

Amy and Asha got out of the car and squinted in the sunlight. There was a man standing with a young boy by a boating shed, and it took Amy a while to click that the man was Rafael Badillo himself. It was strange to see him like this, looking at home and dressed down, like a normal and unglamorous guy.

He waved, but his eyes avoided Asha as they walked over, Asha several steps behind Amy and practically hiding in her shadow.

The little boy mirrored Asha, hiding behind Raf.

'Hey,' Raf said when they got close enough. 'This is my nephew Luis.' He craned backwards at the boy. 'Luis, this is Amy and . . . Asha. You should speak to them in English.'

Luis peered at them from around Raf's leg and then said something to Raf in Spanish.

Raf looked embarrassed. 'Yeah, OK, unless you say things

like that.' He turned to Amy and Asha. 'I hope you don't mind him tagging along, but he's the reason I'm not at the soccer match today. It's just starting now, isn't it?'

Amy nodded.

'I would have taken Luis, but my sister wouldn't allow it. And the baby's ill, so she thought Lu could spend the day with me and practise his English –'

'Swim!' Luis said. He tugged at Raf's sleeve.

'Not now. First we need to go on a boat trip,' Raf explained patiently.

'Swim,' Luis insisted.

Raf started walking. 'Lu, come on, quickly. They're in a rush. They want to talk to Asha's sister. She's on a boat she borrowed from Uncle Raul.'

The boy repeated the phrase he said before.

Asha narrowed her eyes. 'Hold on, what did he say? Did I hear him say "Rena"? Isn't that the name of the girl you were going to marry – the one you dumped when a certain singer called Rosay Sands appeared on the scene?'

Raf stopped and his eyes darkened. 'Asha, not here. We've talked about this.'

'Why not here? Hey, maybe I can ask your nephew if it's true what you told me about that girl leaving you and not the other way round, and about the Rosay thing being all for the press, for your image. Or whether you just made that all up because you're a movie star with a huge ego.'

'No, you can't ask him,' Raf said firmly. He looked away and added, 'And if you really want to know, what Luis said was that you seem prettier and nicer than Rena. And I'd say that's true, even though you have a bigger ego than me.' He coughed. 'Now are we going to find your sister or are you going to dredge up old arguments that don't even matter seeing as, oh, you broke up with me and are never going to speak to me again?'

Asha just looked at him, speechless, as he turned and walked away.

Amy shifted awkwardly. 'Come on, Asha.'

Raf stepped expertly on board a smart-looking speedboat. He lifted Luis on too, and held out a hand to Amy. She took it and stumbled on inelegantly, grateful that she'd worn leggings and flats today.

Then Raf held out a hand to Asha, which she ignored. She landed on deck in an undignified heap, picking herself up and brushing herself off before she sat at the other side of the boat.

Luis stared at her and then at Amy. Amy smiled at him. He frowned at her for ages, but eventually he smiled back.

The engine roared and Raf shouted to make himself heard above the noise. 'There are three main beaches in the area. Two are pretty safe, good swimming beaches; calm waters, beautiful sand. The third is more risky. It's a surfers' beach but it can have treacherous rip tides, even though they've added a breakwater to make it safer.'

Asha was pretending not to listen to him, but Amy saw her bite her lip nervously.

'Maybe we should look around there first, if you're worried about Susi not being able to swim well.'

'Swim!' Luis said.

'Later, Lu,' Raf told him. 'Susi's not on her own, though, is she? Isn't Josh a strong swimmer either?'

'Swim! Swim!' Luis said.

Amy smiled at the boy. The sea looked deep blue and gorgeous and she wouldn't mind a swim either.

'Later, Lu,' Raf said again.

The boat picked up speed and Raf steered it masterfully through the waves. Now that Raf's back was turned, Amy noticed Asha gazing at him the whole time and she wanted to roll her eyes. Her friend could be so incredibly stubborn.

They neared a wide expanse of shoreline where the waves seemed wilder. It was the tail end of siesta time in San Sebastian and the beach was quiet. The lifeguard station was unmanned and a red flag was flying, but there were a few surfers dotted around despite that. There were also a couple of speedboats resting some distance from the beach.

Asha jumped up. 'Is it any of those, Raf? Your brother's boat, I mean?'

Rafael killed the engine. 'So what you really meant was that you'd never speak to me again unless it suits you?'

Asha glared at Raf. 'I thought you wanted to help me.'

Raf shrugged. 'I thought I *was* helping.'

Asha made a 'huh' sound, and Rafael glared at her.

Amy smiled at Luis again, wishing Asha and Raf would get on with it.

'Swim!' said Luis.

'You're impossible,' Raf said quietly to Asha.

Asha raised her voice. '*You're* impossible!'

This time Amy did roll her eyes. She busied herself scanning the beach area for signs of Susi or Josh and tried to tune out the argument that was heating up in front of her.

Rafael's voice was getting quieter and Asha's was getting louder with every line they threw at each other.

Eventually she could only hear Asha, and then she couldn't even hear her, as the unmistakeable whirring of a helicopter filled the air. Amy wondered if someone was in trouble, as Raf had warned.

But it wasn't a rescue helicopter. It was heading right for them.

Paparazzi.

'Oh, great. Have they come for you?' Asha yelled at Raf. 'Because you're so important! And so special! And so FAMOUS!'

Raf just looked disbelievingly at the sky. 'I don't think so. They wouldn't have known I was here.'

'Rubbish! They always know where to find you! Like that day at the beach party!'

Raf shook his head. 'Rosay's PR called them that day. How many times do I have to tell you we were posing for publicity shots? But today . . . I don't get it. Only my family know I'm here.'

A feeling of dread gripped Amy's stomach. Raf was right. How could the paps know they were here? And why had they come? Were they trying to get gossip about Rafael Badillo?

Amy didn't think so. There was nothing particularly scandalous about Rafael being seen with his nephew and Asha right now. She strongly suspected it was about *her*. When they'd arrived in San Sebastian, the England match was just starting. It would be in full flow right now. And she wasn't there. She was going to get papped out 'enjoying herself' while her boyfriend played a nerve-racking match for England. She was going to get blamed – yet again – for not supporting him. There were going to be pictures of her sitting on a boat with a film star and a friend, living it up like the shallow, waste-of-space footballer's girlfriend the press had decided she was.

So who could have called the paps? Assuming Raf's family hadn't told anyone, and knowing she'd only told Rosay, then . . .

It had to be Lauren. Lauren must have guessed what they were doing from the conversation they'd had at Café Biarritz. So she probably did still have her text hotline to Claudette. And Claudette had sent the paps. It seemed far-fetched, but possible.

The helicopter circled overhead. It made Amy so angry! She thought about making a rude gesture or something at it, and then she realized that would make everything worse. She sighed.

Asha was still yelling at Raf. But they were getting closer to each other – despite the paparazzi, which they seemed to be ignoring now. Or maybe they were getting closer because of the helicopter, to make themselves heard above the noise. Either way, the closer they got, the more they were staring into each other's eyes. In fact, if Amy didn't know better, she'd think they were about to kiss. She almost laughed. Raf had been so determined not to talk about his personal life in front of his nephew, and now he looked like he was about to fall into a passionate embrace with Asha, with Luis sitting right –

Amy's blood ran cold.

Where was Luis? She looked around. It was a simple speedboat – there was nowhere to hide.

Luis wasn't on the boat.

'Luis!' she called. Panic struck her. 'Luis! Luis!'

She thought she heard a boy's voice say, 'Swim!' but she wasn't sure because the helicopter noise was deafening. Anger took over her panic and she stood up, making the boat sway.

And then she saw him. Luis, in the sea, in the direction of the shore. Flailing. In trouble.

She screamed at him, 'Luis! Oh my God, hang on!'

She vaguely registered Asha and Raf turn towards her in surprise, but she didn't hear what they said to her as she kicked off her shoes and plunged into the water, swimming with firm strokes towards the little boy, using all her life-guard skills to reach him. She held him, he was safe –

Until she felt it. A suction, like a vacuum cleaner, pulling her and Luis out to sea with a strength she couldn't fight against. Luis panicked against her, struggling against the powerful force, exhausting himself immediately, threatening to break away from her and into treacherous deeper waters.

For about a minute – though it felt much longer – she panicked too. She kicked at the waves, over and over. Her legs started to tire and her body felt heavy and useless. Her head bobbed under the water. Luis clung to her neck, sputtering and pushing her down.

Then she surfaced, took a deep breath and let her life-guard training flood back to her, filling her head with calm.

She corrected her tight hold on Luis, saying soothing things to him until he relaxed in her grip. She stopped fighting against the tide and let the ocean carry them for a while, until they were beyond the breakwater. As Amy swam parallel to the shore, the water around her seemed to relax too. She headed smoothly for land, where she lay Luis down on the beach. She got ready to administer first aid, but he sat up straight away and threw his arms round her in a hug, and she hugged him back. She'd never felt more relieved in all her life.

The helicopters swooped towards them and by the time Asha and Raf were on the beach with them – Raf immediately picking his nephew up and holding him tightly – Amy realized she must have had about a million pictures taken. Her clothes were wet through and she was shivering despite the heat of sun, and she was certain there were all kinds of mean things the press could say about the way she looked right now.

But they could say whatever they liked. She absolutely didn't care, and she didn't think she ever would again.

22

When the fuss had died down and they'd beaten off a sudden swarm of reporters, Raf said he needed to get Luis home and he insisted that Amy should go with him to get a change of clothes. He said he could arrange for a friend to take Asha back out in his boat to keep looking for Susi, and she agreed gratefully. He'd left the boat nearby, moored hastily to the breakwater in their hurry to reach Luis.

'I'm really sorry, Raf,' Asha said after he made the call. 'If I hadn't distracted you – I mean . . .'

'No, it was my fault.' He squeezed her shoulder, but didn't move closer to her. 'But thanks. Hope your sister's OK,' he said. 'Mine's going to kill me. Give us a call as soon as you have any news.'

Then he nodded to Amy, picked up Luis and carried the little boy slowly back to his house.

Raf's sister, Maia, was horrified when she saw them and heard what had happened. She cried and hugged her son, and then Amy. Then she raced around running warm baths and arranging changes of clothes and generally making Amy feel totally welcome. Best of all, when she'd calmed down a bit, she told Amy that England had won their match today.

'Just one goal, but a good one. By that very handsome Danny Harris.'

A long while later they were settled round a table in the massive kitchen, drinking hot chocolate and eating delicious snacks, and Amy listened as Raf's sister chatted.

'I'm so glad to meet you. I've read a lot about you on the online gossip sites. I used to read them to find out about my brother, but now I'm completely hooked and I never miss a twist in the lives of any of you celebrities!' she said.

'Oh no, I'm not a celebrity,' Amy said.

Maia laughed. 'Of course you are. We all want to know about everything you wear, and your every move! I'll tell you what, though. I knew it wasn't true, all that terrible stuff they've been saying about you. I knew you seemed good and kind, even before Raf said you were friends with his new girlfriend.'

'Maia, I told you Asha and I are not together any more,' Raf said quickly.

'That's what they all say. Like that latest scandal online with the football manager's daughter and that English player who plays in Spain now. What's his name? Scott?'

'Scott White? You read something about Scott White online?' Amy asked, instantly worried for Rosay. Had Lauren spread *that* gossip already too?

'Yes, Scott White, that's it. And Rosay Sands, the singer with the famous family and the glamorous mother who looks twenty years younger than me! They're having a secret relationship.' She laughed. 'I'm always up to date with the latest celebrity news! Raf hates it.'

Amy's mind raced, wondering if that was why Rosay had

sounded so strange on the phone earlier. Maybe she hadn't mentioned it because she didn't want to worry Amy, under the circumstances? Poor Rosay – she'd tried so hard to keep Scott a secret.

Maia moved away from the subject of celebrities and started telling funny stories about her brothers and the things they used to get up to as children. Meanwhile, Raf played with Luis in the background, pausing to add the occasional comment like, 'Don't listen to her!' and 'That's not true!'

They were interrupted by Raf's phone ringing. He took the call outside, leaving Maia raising her eyebrows.

'Girlfriend trouble again, I bet,' she remarked. 'My brother needs more of the movie star ego. He's too soft and girls keep breaking his heart. Don't tell him I told you that!'

After a bit more chatting, Amy smiled and excused herself, thinking she'd check her phone too, but she realized quickly that she didn't have it. She'd left her bag on the boat.

Amy was hesitating in the kitchen doorway when Raf came back in with relief written all over his face.

'That was Asha. Susi's OK!'

'Really? Oh, thank God!' Amy felt like hugging him. 'Where was she? Where has she been? What happened to her?'

'That's just it.' Raf smiled. 'Absolutely nothing! Susi has been with her boyfriend on Isla Santa Clara – that's a tiny island just off the bay, and the mobile phone reception can be patchy around there. Anyway, they were having a picnic. They were travelling back to Barcelona tonight. There was really nothing to worry about.' Raf frowned. 'She's pretty dramatic, isn't she? Asha, I mean?'

'Um, yeah, she can be,' Amy mumbled. Though she herself was a still a bit shocked that Susi would take off like that in the first place – especially overnight, and without telling her sister. She wondered whether Susi really was paying them back for all the times she and Asha called Susi 'sensible' and made it sound like she could never do anything daring or adventurous.

Raf had a misty look on his face – clearly thinking about Asha. 'I bet she'd do well in the movie biz.'

Amy groaned. 'God, don't tempt her.'

But Raf didn't smile. Maybe he hadn't been joking. 'Oh, Asha says she has your bag,' he said. 'Sorry we didn't notice we'd left it in the boat. She, um, doesn't want to come here to give it to you.' He avoided Amy's eyes. 'But she asked if you could meet her by the harbour as soon as possible?'

Amy thanked everyone loads, promised to send back Maia's clothes and gave Luis another big hug before she made her way back to the harbour, wondering if she'd ever meet Raf again. Probably not – it didn't look like he and Asha were getting back together. Though it vaguely sounded like Raf might try to get her a role in Hollywood. Amy smiled to herself, thinking that Raf was right – Asha would make a fantastic actress. And it would complete Amy's set – footballer boyfriend, pop star friend, movie star friend . . .

That was if she and Damien managed to stay together. She thought she'd better call him as soon as she'd spoken to Asha and Susi and got her phone back. She needed to congratulate him about today, apart from anything else. But he'd probably disapprove of the way she'd taken off to San Sebastian instead of watching him in Bilbao, especially now it turned out that there hadn't been anything to worry about. He'd complain about her giving the paps another opportunity to make her look bad. He might not say it, but he'd think it reflected badly on him. It made her slightly dread ringing him, which she knew was all kinds of wrong.

And then she reached the harbour, and there he was. Damien, standing with Asha and clearly waiting for her.

It was incredibly awkward.

Damien looked at her and she looked back, but neither of them moved to give each other a hug or a kiss or even to stand a tiny bit closer. So Amy hadn't imagined his frostiness last time they'd spoken on the phone, then. Their relationship really was in trouble.

Asha chattered on at length about how she'd found Susi and Josh on the island, enjoying themselves as if there was nothing wrong with having a picnic when everyone was out frantically looking for them. She said she'd really had a go at Susi – on Amy's behalf too. Apparently Susi had got annoyed about that, saying she'd be back in plenty of time for the flight tomorrow and Asha had no right to go spying on her, and it wasn't her fault her phone hadn't worked earlier when they were at sea. Anyway she knew Asha wouldn't have thought twice about taking off like that if *her* boyfriend had offered to take her away for a while. So then Asha had said that her boyfriend *had* offered to take her away, but she'd refused because she had principles, and she used to think Susi did too, and anyway she didn't have a boyfriend any more. It sounded like they'd had a huge row right there in front of Josh. Then Josh had dared to suggest that Asha should leave Susi alone and Asha had shouted at him too and left in a huff.

'Oh, and the minute I was back on the mainland, my phone went, and it was Damien, saying he was here and he'd been trying to call you and did I know where you were? That's when I found your phone on the boat, and I called Raf to tell you to come here. So . . .' Asha finally seemed to notice the way Damien and Amy were behaving. 'Oh no, what's going on? Is there something in the air today? My whole life has gone weird. I've never known you two not be all over each other the second you meet.'

No one said anything. Amy fiddled with edging on the sundress Maia had lent her. It wasn't the kind of thing she'd normally wear. She didn't feel at all like herself. That was her excuse for acting strangely.

What was Damien's?

'OK,' said Asha slowly. 'I think I'll have a wander around the old town. May as well grab all the fun I can, seeing as tomorrow I'm going back to Stanleydale with no boyfriend and a sister I've disowned.' She handed Amy the bag she'd left on the boat. 'Give me a call when you're ready to head back, or whatever.'

She gave them a funny look, then she left Amy and Damien in silence.

'Amy . . .' Damien said after a very long minute. He didn't move any closer to her, though. 'Come on. Let's find somewhere to talk.'

'Yeah,' Amy mumbled. Why exactly had he come here? What could be so important that he'd actually taken time off when he was allowed to?

Amy couldn't help thinking he was about to break up with her.

Her heart pounded at the thought. But she also thought about how she'd come close to breaking up with *him* recently, on the phone. This wouldn't exactly be out of the blue.

They wandered silently through the old town and into a tiny pintxos bar where they sat across from each other at a metal table, under a large black-and-white Picasso-style painting.

At first they ordered snacks and drinks and they talked politely, like they had in the last few texts they'd sent each other. Amy thought they sounded like strangers. It almost felt worse than arguing.

Eventually, Damien took a deep breath and looked like he was about to say what was really on his mind. Amy braced herself.

'You know, Ames . . . I'm so glad you're OK. I heard you nearly drowned. I took a taxi straight here as soon as I got the news.'

Amy should have felt relieved, but she didn't. She suddenly realized she was furious.

She glared at him. 'I'm a trained lifeguard, Damien. I didn't "nearly drown". Who did you hear that from? Was it in the news? That was super-quick. I should have known they wouldn't waste any time when they could be having a go at me!'

'No . . .'

'So is that why you're here?'

'Yes, listen. I –'

'You're here because of some report full of half-truths? That's what it takes to make you finally take time off when you're allowed to spend time with me?'

'No, I . . .'

'You know what, Damien? I don't even care any more about the distorted pictures those paps sell. If they hadn't been hovering above us trying to make me look bad, we'd have heard Raf's nephew jump into the water.'

'Listen . . .'

'It's all messed up. Asha and Raf are blaming themselves, and they'd probably have got back together if the paps hadn't ruined everything. But anyway, it's really *my* fault that little boy was in trouble today. Raf's love life isn't the latest gossip any more. I know it was me they were after.'

'Amy, hang on, you can't blame yourself.'

'Yeah, OK, you're right. I blame *us*. Me and you. They're so busy trying to prove I'm a rubbish girlfriend that they don't care what the fallout is. And everyone thinks you're better off without me.' Her stomach filled with butterflies, but she couldn't stop – not now she'd said this much. '*You* think you're better off without me. Fewer distractions. No one to bring you down or reflect badly on you. And I think . . . I think . . .'

Damien fixed his dark eyes on her, but he didn't say anything.

'I think everyone's right,' she finished. 'So . . .'

'Amy. Don't. You don't want to –'

'No, you're right. I don't want to. And just imagine how heartless everyone would think I was if I . . .' She struggled with the words. 'If I broke up with you,' she managed at last. 'During your first ever World Cup tournament.' She stopped for a moment and stared at the table. 'And anyway I don't want to break up with you.'

'So don't,' Damien said, swallowing hard.

She looked up. 'But it would make things easier for you, wouldn't it? Come on, Damien – I know you've been thinking it.'

'That's not true, Ames!' His voice went quiet. 'OK, I have thought once or twice that it might make things easier for *you*.'

She glared at him.

'No, listen! You know I've always been in two minds about the media stuff you've done, but at least I thought you were enjoying it. But now you're really not – it's caused you nothing but trouble lately, hasn't it? And I know it's not the same as it is for me. I want to be a footballer, I have to accept the media attention that goes with it, don't I? But this isn't what *you* want to do with your life. Fitness DVDs and photo shoots for magazines? Being papped out shopping with girls like Lauren Thompson and Kylie Kemp? Being seen as . . . you know . . . just a footballer's girlfriend. It's not you.'

'What do you know about it? You've barely seen me lately!'

Damien frowned. 'I'm only going on what you've always told me, Ames. And I don't have to see you to know it's been getting you down.' His frown deepened. 'Look, whichever

202

way you look at it, you didn't ask for all this. You know, all the bad stuff in the press. It's got worse because I'm playing for England, hasn't it? So, yeah, it's my fault. And, yeah, I've been thinking you might be better off doing your own thing. Out of the spotlight, I mean.' He lowered his eyes. 'Back in Stanleydale.'

Amy felt another flash of anger. 'So you *want* me to go?'

'I'm thinking of *you*, Ames! When Rosay told me all that stuff, I realized just how bad things had got for you.'

'Wait a minute – when did you speak to Rosay?'

'She was at this after-match thing today with her step-dad and Trina – she'd just come from some event nearby, I think. She came straight over when she saw me and she told me that Susi was missing and you'd got into trouble at sea trying to find her. Among other things. I came as quick as I could to see if I could help.' He reached a hand towards her. 'And to see you.'

She didn't take his hand. 'Rosay told you where we were? You didn't hear it in the news, or whatever?'

'She heard it from her dad. The pictures came in at his agency. I bet it *will* make the news, though. Sounds like you were really brave, Ames.'

But Amy wasn't listening to Damien any more.

She was thinking.

Rosay knew where Amy was. She was the only one who did. She'd made all the arrangements with the private plane and everything.

Amy's heart sank. Rosay used to 'spy' for Claudette a long time ago. Plus she knew photographers – lots of them.

Her dad was a photography agent. Could *she* have called the paps today?

No, she couldn't have. Rosay was a friend. Wasn't she? Why would she do a thing like this? Amy wracked her brains.

Then she remembered what Raf's sister had said about Scott White. How she'd read gossip online about how Rosay was seeing Scott. And Amy had forgotten to warn Rosay about Lauren. Could Rosay have thought that Amy revealed her secret about Scott? Had she sent out the paps as a revenge move against Amy because of that?

Anyway, it was too late. Whatever had happened, and whatever the reason, Amy knew she wouldn't feel comfortable staying at Rosay's house now. She didn't feel like confronting Rosay, either. What was the point in going through all that if Damien didn't even want her here? Let Rosay believe what she wanted. Amy wasn't sure she could ever forgive her for sending out the paps like that anyway, and putting a boy's life in danger.

Damien was right. She should just forget this whole crazy celebrity life thing, with all its scandals and games and tricks, and enemies disguised as friends. She didn't want it. It was damaging and stressful and it wasn't *her*.

'Amy? Are you OK?'

'No. No, I'm not, but don't worry about it. Look, I don't think we should talk about this any more – not right now, anyway. I'm going to find Asha, and we'll make our own way back to Barcelona. And tomorrow I'll fly back to Stanleydale with the twins. I'm going home. And look, don't call me or text me – I don't want to distract you, OK? You should focus on the football, like you've been saying all along.' Her voice choked a bit as she added, 'Bye, Damien. Good luck.'

Her chair made a horrible scraping noise on the marble floor as she got up and walked out of the bar.

23

Amy had been back in England for well over a week when her dad forced her to look at one of the papers she'd been desperately avoiding.

She'd actually been avoiding a lot of things. Newspapers were one. Online gossip sites and blogs, definitely, were another. She wouldn't watch the news on television, just in case. She avoided the living room because her dad seemed to be watching non-stop football coverage. She wouldn't walk past Damien's family's house next door, even though it was empty. But it made her sad just to look at the house and remember all the times she'd popped over to see her boyfriend – before he was famous.

She was obsessive about screening messages and calls on her phone. She'd sent Rosay a very short message saying she wasn't staying, but not explaining why, and at first she'd had a few calls and messages back. But she didn't answer and she deleted the texts without reading them. She didn't want to get drawn into a blame game.

She also ignored frequent calls from her publicist. Even if it wasn't true that he was only working for Claudette, he was only going to make her think about the thing she'd been avoiding so desperately – the media. He'd probably be full of plans to rescue her image – or make it worse. She wasn't interested.

She replied to calls and texts from Asha and Susi, though, and she saw them too. Susi was still with Josh, even though she hadn't seen him since she'd got back because he was in London and she hadn't thought of a mum-proof excuse to visit. Asha wasn't back with Raf and was sure she never would be. Worst of all, the twins still weren't talking to each other, so Amy always had to do stuff with them one at a time, as ridiculous as that felt.

Life back in Stanleydale was proving to be pretty miserable.

And Damien hadn't got in touch with her at all. Amy knew she'd specifically asked him not to call her, but it still hurt that he'd taken her at her word. She herself was wrestling daily with the urge to call or text him, and especially when she'd sneaked into the living room and watched England win the quarter-finals and then – amazingly – the semi-final too. Damien hadn't played in the first match, but she'd caught a glimpse of him on the subs bench. He'd played the final half hour of the semis, though, looking fantastic, if a bit nervous. But he'd helped set up the winning goal and Amy didn't think anyone but her would have noticed his nerves on the pitch. She'd fought particularly hard not to text him then, as she watched him on telly and joined with her dad in cheering him on. After the match she hadn't been able to resist any longer, and she sent Damien a message of congratulations. It ended in a long row of kisses and, as an afterthought because she didn't want to put pressure on him, she wrote: 'Don't reply!'

After that, she'd stared at her blank phone all night, until she felt completely stupid and wished she could take the whole message back.

The next morning, her dad cornered her by the kettle, wielding the paper and waving it in front of her face like he meant business.

'Amy, you have to see this,' he said.

'Is it about how brilliantly Damien played last night?' She took the paper out of his hands and rested it on the counter top. 'Thanks, Dad, I'll have a look later,' she lied. She tried to change the subject. 'Did you want tea?'

But her dad had never been easily distracted. 'Your lad did us proud, Amy – and whatever happens, I'll probably always think of Damien as your lad. Anyway, you need to read that paper.'

'Oh, Dad!' Amy sighed. She knew he meant well, and she wanted to be honest. 'I'm sorry, I don't want to. I'm a bit upset about this stuff right now. I'm starting to think I shouldn't even have watched last night's match.'

'Course you should have! Even if Damien hadn't played, it was still your country getting through to the World Cup final. It's huge!'

Amy busied herself making tea.

'Besides, it's not all about Damien. There's quite a lot in the paper about you, love.'

'Oh,' Amy said, her heart sinking. It was exactly what she wanted to avoid. What were they accusing her of now? Being a traitor to the England team because she'd gone home? What did they know about her life, anyway?

Her dad shook his head. 'Look, I know you're having a rough time with all this, but if you read all the bad things they said before, then you have to see this too.' He tapped at the newspaper and left her alone in the kitchen with it.

Amy pushed the mugs aside and glanced at the front-page headline that promised: *'Read about Angel Amy inside!'* Then she did a double take and looked again. She flicked to the page about her and read it carefully, twice, to make sure she wasn't imagining it.

The press had done a complete about-turn. There were amazingly flattering pictures of her, underlined with captions full of admiration. The story was completely over-the-top, but in a good way for a change. *'She's a lifesaver!'* one pull-out quote screamed, and 'The People's Comment' below it called her *'Britain's own Amy Thornton'*, as if she somehow belonged to the country now, rather than shaming the nation with her so-called *'antics'* like she had two weeks before. Even in the sports pages it said: *'Damien shines for England after Angel Amy saves a boy's life!'*

After a while, her dad poked his head round the kitchen door. 'See what I mean?' he said. 'It's not the first one I've seen like that, either. Everyone's talking about you at work. And I told you I saw that footage on telly of you saving the kid.' He smiled at her. 'You're a national heroine.'

'Dad,' Amy said. 'I don't want to be.'

'OK, fair enough. I just wanted you to know that you don't have to hide in Stanleydale, whatever's going on between you and Damien.' He took a deep breath. 'Your mother tells me there's a footballer's wedding the day after the cup final. One of your new mates.'

'Oh, yeah. Kylie's marrying Johaan Haag.'

'The Netherlands? They got knocked out by Brazil on Tuesday.'

'Yeah, I know.' Amy hoped Kylie and Johann were OK. She sort of missed them, actually – and Poshie too. Some of those people out in Spain were definitely her friends. Kylie, for one. Trina too – she'd gone out of her way to help out, and Amy wondered how her plan to get at Claudette and Lauren was going, and whether she needed any help. She realized she hadn't even thanked her for stopping the horrible texts.

Maybe she'd give them a call soon. After all, she couldn't cut herself off from the football world completely. It would always feel like part of her life.

She was thinking about all this so hard that she almost missed what her dad was saying.

'So your mother wants to pay for you to go to the wedding.' He smiled indulgently. 'Between you and me, I think she wants to see a picture of you in her magazine, wearing some fancy glad rags.' He shrugged. 'I told her we can just dress you up here and take a pic with the old camera, but she's behaving like that's not the same.'

'Oh, Dad, I don't know about going back out there . . .' Rosay would be there. And Damien. She wasn't sure she wanted to face either of them yet – especially Damien. She and Damien had been invited to the wedding as a couple. It would be heartbreaking to turn up alone. And – her mind raced – Paige would be there. Kylie had been fairly sure of that. Amy was sure that Paige had always had a thing for Damien. What if . . .

'OK, tell you what.' Amy's dad interrupted her thoughts. 'Don't go for the wedding.'

'Oh.' Amy felt a sudden weird disappointment, despite what she'd been thinking. 'OK.'

'No. Go for the World Cup final. It's the day before the wedding.' He gave a satisfied nod. 'We can get you a return for a few days later, and book you into a B&B. So you might be a bit bored and fancy popping along to Johann Haag's do. You know. Posh grub and a bit of a knees-up, and all that. I didn't want to go to your Auntie June's wedding either, you know, but it was worth it in the end for the cheap bar and the karaoke.'

'Dad!'

'Course, this wedding is bound to be classier than Auntie June's.' He grinned. 'You might even have a *free* bar.'

Amy thought guiltily about her cancelled DVD. 'Seriously, Dad, what about the money?'

'Your mum says the wedding's near Malaga – very convenient for the final. I think we can stretch to one of those cheapie flights, a budget B&B and some spending money for when you go out with those wealthy friends of yours. You can pay us back one day. You know, when you're a famous physiotherapist.'

'I'd rather just be a normal physiotherapist,' Amy said, her mind already halfway to the twins' house so they could help her pick out something to wear to the footballers' wedding of the century. In fact, if she argued with them both about it in just the right way, she was sure she'd be able to reunite the twins over it.

24

Amy's plan worked a treat and Asha and Susi – together – saw Amy off at the airport. She hugged them tightly, meaning every word she said as she told them how much she wished they were travelling with her.

'We couldn't,' Asha said drily. 'Stanleydale needs us. We add a touch of much-needed glamour to our grey town.'

'Mum's got us on a lead,' Susi sighed. 'Have a brilliant time. Tell Damien we said hello.'

'I don't know if I'll be speaking to him,' Amy said sadly, and she noticed the twins exchange a strange glance, as if they'd been discussing Damien, but they weren't going to share what they'd said with Amy. It could have been annoying, but Amy was so glad they were talking to each other again that she didn't care.

In the departure lounge, Amy caught a glimpse of Damien on a large screen as some sports programme gave a run-through of England's progress to the World Cup final. She took out her phone and wrote him a text that said: 'I'm coming to Spain!'

Then she deleted it, thinking of the way he hadn't replied after the semi-final.

Arriving in Spain alone was slightly nerve-racking. Amy clutched the hotel details her mum had written out for her on a piece of paper, telling herself this wouldn't be difficult. She didn't even really need the paper – her dad had already given the address to the taxi firm he'd booked to meet her from the plane. She stared intently at the row of signs held by the drivers at the arrivals gate, scouring them for her name. But she couldn't find it. She started to panic slightly.

And then she saw him. Damien. The real Damien – not some picture on television.

He'd had come to meet her at the airport, the same way she had when he'd first arrived to play for England, and hiding under a similar baseball cap.

She stifled an instinct to jump for joy. Instead she stopped in front of him as a nervous smile twitched on his face.

'Damien,' she said. 'Hello.'

'Hi, Amy.' He moved towards her, but she stepped back, unsure, and his smile wavered even more.

Why was he here? 'How did you know to meet me from this plane?'

Damien shrugged. 'Asha and Susi. They sent me a message a couple of days ago. Asha said I'd better be here or else.'

That explained it, but Amy wasn't sure how it made her feel. It was fantastic to see Damien again. But he'd only come because Asha had threatened him, or something. And, worse, the awkwardness she'd felt around him in San Sebastian hadn't gone away. She clutched her holdall, keeping her hands busy so that she didn't give in to the urge to throw her arms round him. Although that temptation was fading with every passing second of him shifting nervously as if he didn't want to be there.

He glanced around. 'Your driver's here too.' He nodded in the direction of an unshaven man holding a sign that said 'Amy Thornton', right at the end of the cluster of drivers. 'I had to make sure I stood over here so you saw me first.'

'Oh. So you're not here to . . .' Amy didn't want to finish that sentence, because it sounded a bit pathetic.

'Take you to your hotel?'

And now Amy thought it sounded completely stupid.

'I can't, I'm sorry.' He stared at the ground. 'I've only got about half an hour before training starts, you know, and it's –'

'It's the World Cup final tomorrow.' Amy's eyes widened at the enormity of it. 'I can't believe you're even here.' Why had he bothered to come, if he had no time to see her? What was this about?

'I wanted to get things straight as soon as possible. I've got something I really need to say to you – something I don't want to talk about over the phone.' He gulped. 'I've been thinking about everything. Listen, I think I can't – We can't –'

There was a sudden scuffle and a photographer appeared in front of them, snapping like crazy.

Amy stifled a groan. She almost wished Damien hadn't come here. Now she was more confused about him than ever, and they couldn't even manage two minutes of privacy for him to finish a sentence. It was useless.

'Damien, thanks for coming, but you should probably go to training,' she said quietly.

'But . . .'

Another photographer appeared.

Amy shielded her eyes from the camera. 'You should just do your thing and win the World Cup for England, OK? I know you can. You're amazing.'

She found her driver and walked away, half of her wishing she hadn't said that last part at all, if their relationship was over. And the other half wanting to turn back right now and do everything she could to make things OK between them again.

The World Cup final crowd was the biggest Amy had ever seen and the excited atmosphere swelled into every corner of the stadium. Amy stood at the back of the family and friends area on her own, mostly because she'd arrived late to avoid running into Lauren or any of the others. She didn't feel like joining in with the gossip right now – or being the subject of it.

It was also partly because she felt a bit like she had no right to be there, even though she'd had no problem getting in. Was she still Damien's girlfriend?

She stood through the national anthems and her worries started to fade. It was impossible not to get swept along with the roar that followed the last notes. Soon the whistle had blown and the England–Brazil match was underway.

At first, Damien wasn't on the pitch and Amy tried not to think about how disappointed he'd be to have missed out on this opportunity. But just before the second half, Brazil scored and, shortly afterwards, Vulkan made a substitution in mid-field. And he was on – Damien Taylor was playing in the World Cup final. Amy knew it was a dream come true for him.

He played like a superstar. He covered the pitch at speed and wherever the ball was, Damien wasn't far behind. Still, the other team weren't exactly amateurs, and it was nearly the end of the second half before a series of excellent passes – one of which was by Damien – led to England's equalizer.

After that, time really started to drag, even though it was completely action-packed. There were so many near-misses on both sides that Amy found herself clutching her hand to her mouth, but there were no more goals. It was all going to be decided on penalties.

There was a never-ending amount of what looked to Amy like messing about at the side of the pitch, and then a nail-biting hush fell on the crowd as the players stepped up, one by one, to take their penalties.

Brazil went first. They were four–three up when it was England's turn again. And Amy nearly gasped when she saw it was Damien stepping on to the pitch.

There was a rumble of voices in front of her. They said things like, 'What's Vulkan thinking?' and 'Didn't he miss his last penno?'

At first, Amy covered her eyes and peered through her fingers at the pitch. But Damien's strides were filled with confidence and Amy took her hand away. She had to see this.

He glanced up at the crowd and she wondered whether there was any way he could see her. She beamed out a smile just in case, willing him on with every bone in her body. She was sure the cameras were picking her out, but she didn't care – she brushed off the feeling of being watched and focused on what was happening on the pitch.

Damien took a run-up and belted the ball.

Right into the back of the net. The goalie didn't stand a chance.

Amy shook the stands with her cheering.

But the euphoria on Amy's side of the stadium was short-lived. Brazil got their next penalty and then there was a tense silence as the next England player stepped forward.

He faltered as he kicked the ball right at the Brazilian goalie – who caught it expertly.

The England player sank to the ground and a stunned lull fell around Amy.

England had lost the World Cup final on penalties.

Amy joined in with the mourning that hit the England supporters within seconds. They were all devastated.

A tiny part of Amy couldn't help thinking about Damien's goal, though. She wondered what it must have taken for him to stand up in front of the nation who had rubbished him pretty severely after he'd missed his previous penalty. And yet he'd done it. She also knew how much sympathy he'd feel for the player who'd failed to get a penalty just now. Damien was a team player through and through.

Amy knew Damien was unreachable on the pitch, but she still ached to find him and throw her arms round him. She wondered if she ever would again.

25

By mid-afternoon the next day, most England supporters had shrugged off their loss and turned it into in-depth play-by-play analysis, often accompanied by drinking sessions that started off mournful and ended up as huge parties.

Amy herself felt like she was at one of the biggest parties in the world. Kylie hadn't been joking when she said she'd be having a fairy-tale wedding. She'd hired an authentic Spanish castle, and it was amazing. It stood on a hill, casting awesome shadows over the countryside below. The view was incredible too – there didn't seem to be a house for miles, and just beyond a cluster of rugged mountains, the Andalucían coast twinkled in the distance.

The castle had been adapted to cater for every luxury. The rooms were intricately and tastefully decorated and the waiters wandered about in smart uniforms, discreetly offering champagne to the guests.

And it was just as well, because Amy couldn't help thinking that that was where all the taste and discretion stopped. Absolutely everything else about the day was proving to be over-the-top, overblown and, well, bordering on tacky. It was also pretty good fun. And the *Just Gossip* team couldn't get enough of it. There were photographers and journalists everywhere.

First, all the guests and press had gathered in the enormous courtyard and watched Kylie arrive riding side-saddle on a white stallion, her hair newly extended to cascade in ringlets down one shoulder, dripping with jewels and topped with a large tiara. It took three people to help her dismount and hurriedly rearrange the billowing tiers of her dress. The horse was pulling a carriage containing a gaggle of cute bridesmaids, all children in flamboyant gold gowns, which had obviously been bought before the change of plans. One of the girls was holding Poshie, who was fully kitted out in his golden pageboy – or rather page *dog* – outfit. When Kylie stepped regally up the aisle through the rows of seated guests he followed her, head held high, causing several people to say 'Aw'. Until he stopped and raised his leg by one of the guests' chairs. Kylie turned round and hissed, 'Poshie! You're so embarrassing!' and the guest in question laughed politely. The bridesmaids nearly fell over with laughter.

Then Kylie and Johann exchanged their vows, which were poems they'd written themselves, and it was the guests' turn to be embarrassed and stifle helpless laughs. Amy noticed more than one member of the wedding party developing a fierce attack of the giggles and having to disguise it as a coughing fit. By the time Kylie and Johann kissed theatrically – with Johann sweeping his bride down low in his arms as if they were flamenco dancing – nearly every member of the wedding party was either staring in horror or sounding like they'd caught a sudden bad cold.

It was a relief to gather in the enormous banqueting hall

and raid the gorgeous-looking buffet as slushy love songs blared through the loudspeakers. Amy helped herself to food and wandered about nervously, unsure who to stand with or talk to. She'd spotted Lauren Thompson earlier – without Steve – and she thought she'd seen Trina Santos too, but other than that she didn't recognize many people. It seemed like a lot of Kylie's friends were late or weren't coming, unless Amy just hadn't seen them in the crowds. There didn't seem to be any sign of Rosay, or even Paige. And, though she'd scanned the room for him a million times, Amy couldn't see Damien anywhere.

Then again, Danny Harris wasn't there either. Maybe the England boys had decided not to come – she'd seen on the news that the team was busy in the hotel bar, bonding over their loss. She tried not to feel disappointed. It would have been awkward to see Damien anyway, when things were still so unsure between them. Or possibly when things were over between them – she had to face it. Their last conversations certainly seemed to suggest it.

Then someone behind her screeched a loud, 'Amy! Hello!' and Amy was surprised when she turned round and recognized – though barely – Courtney, Steve's ex. Courtney had changed a bit in the past year – she had a deep, authentic-looking tan, golden hair extensions and bags of confidence Amy didn't remember her having before.

Then she was doubly amazed to notice that Steve was walking towards them, carrying drinks that were obviously meant for him and Courtney.

'Hi babe,' he said, handing one drink to Courtney and kissing her passionately right in front of Amy. 'Oh, and you,

Amy. You made it, then? Us Boroughs boys were allowed to escape Joe Vulkan's clutches for Johann's big day, just for a few hours. The gaffer doesn't really approve of us being at the wedding of a Dutch International!' He laughed. 'Hey, Damien's probably off with Paige somewhere. I'll tell him you're here.' He blew them both kisses and walked off.

Amy resisted an urge to run after him and kill him, or at least question him about Paige, and then she reminded herself about what Damien said. Steve was all gossip – he was a male version of Lauren.

Except, of course, he was back with Courtney now.

Courtney laughed. 'Don't worry, I haven't even seen Paige here.'

Amy wanted to ask whether she'd seen Damien, though, and if so – where? But instead she watched as Courtney leant towards her and clinked glasses. 'To me and Steve. Isn't it great that we're back together?'

'Oh. Er, yeah,' Amy said, vaguely wondering what any girl saw in Steve. Except wealth, of course. And arrogance.

She looked over at Lauren, standing in a corner eating on her own. Courtney followed her gaze and lowered her voice, 'Do you want to know what I did? In case you need it. You know . . . to split up Damien and Paige. They might even be together right now.'

Amy looked at her. 'I thought you said Paige wasn't here?'

'Well, I don't know for sure. And where's Damien? Anyway, I'm just saying. Between you and me . . . It was easy. The only hard bit was getting hold of Lauren's number. But I managed to steal it from Rosay's phone when we were at her party. I had to do it quick, though

– I've never copied down a number so fast in my life! But the rest was easy.'

Amy started feeling distinctly *un*easy.

'What are you talking about? What did you do?'

'Nothing bad. Honestly! I just sent Lauren some messages telling her what I thought. You know, how she was bringing Steve down, how she should leave him . . . I didn't even have to send many! By the knockout rounds, she'd completely given in and, you know, knocked him out or whatever. Apparently she told him she suspected him of cheating because she'd seen some of my texts to *him*. Funny, huh? I didn't think she knew my number, but it turns out she did, so she knew it was me texting her. Anyway, who cares? I stepped right back in where I left off with Steve. Simple.'

Amy stared at her. Those nasty texts sounded a lot like the messages *she'd* got. It was impossible, though.

Unless . . . were those messages meant for Lauren? Were they from Courtney after all, and about Steve?

'There's no need to look at me like that.' Courtney sniffed. 'Steve only really wants to be with me. It was going to happen anyway.'

'Sorry . . . where did you say you got the number? Lauren's number, I mean?'

Courtney laughed. 'At party at Carlo di Rossi's house, after I had a huge row with Lauren and I saw Rosay's phone just lying around. She had all the WAG numbers listed alphabetically by surname – she's so organized! It's all: "Lauren Thompson, Amy Thornton, Paige Young". I was in a mad rush copying down the number because Rosay was already stalking about looking for her phone, but I managed it. Then

I dumped the phone in the laundry room and no one suspected a thing. Genius, eh? So let me know if you want help with . . . you know, getting Paige away from Damien.' She looked excitedly at the stage. 'Ooh, here comes Rosay now.'

Amy watched as Rosay appeared on stage, microphone in hand, but she could barely concentrate as Rosay's voice filled the hall.

Courtney must have copied down the wrong number in her rush! She'd got Amy's number instead of Lauren's – it was the only explanation! So Courtney was the anonymous texter – the one that made her doubt her relationship with Damien. It had all been a wrong number after all. How could things have got so mixed-up?

Not that it excused Courtney. She and Lauren were as bad as each other! She glanced at the corner Lauren had been in, and noticed she'd disappeared. And Steve wasn't back yet either. She shook her head inwardly – she didn't trust them at all. Hadn't Damien told her that Steve was seeing both Lauren and Courtney at one stage?

'Look, I'm just nipping out for a sec. See you in a bit,' Courtney told Amy and she slipped off, probably looking for Steve.

Amy tried to feel sorry for her, but it was hard after what she'd just heard. It was equally hard to feel sorry for Lauren, who was a total trouble-maker.

It was weird that Trina had been so sure the texts were from Claudette, though. Amy looked over at where Trina was standing by the stage, watching Rosay perform. Trina obviously wasn't as reliable a walking phone directory as she'd made out.

Rosay finished the song she was singing and said into the microphone, 'Hello, Kylie and Johann's wedding party! It's great to be here!'

A couple of people cheered.

'I hope you're enjoying yourselves! There will be speeches from the bride and groom soon, including more poems.'

Amy thought she heard someone groan.

'But there's something I really want to say first. I don't want it to take away from what Kylie Kemp – I mean, Mrs Haag – has to say, because that really is very important. But I've cleared this with Kylie and she says it's OK. Plus I really want to announce it in front of my friends. Even the friends who've gone off me for one reason or another.'

A few people laughed then, but Rosay's eyes caught Amy's, and Amy had a feeling she was serious. She wondered whether Rosay was going to try to excuse herself for what she'd done to Amy in San Sebastian – but she didn't exactly see how she could. Calling the paps that day nearly caused a real tragedy, not just a bunch of nasty gossip in the papers. Amy would never find it easy to forgive.

Rosay cleared her throat. 'Yes, I've got used to a certain person standing on tables and making gossip-filled speeches at various parties, and I thought this time it was my turn!'

She laughed, and Amy noticed a few people look at Trina, who did have a habit of making big announcements at parties. Amy had witnessed a couple of them in the past.

'Yes, ladies and gentlemen, members of the press, and all you *Just Gossip* journalists out there . . . Weddings are all about love. Unconditional, accepting love – the sort that exists for all the right reasons, the sort that it's hard to deny.

Even though I was denying it, for the longest time. I was seeing someone in secret, pretending it wasn't happening, for the sake of my image. Until someone announced it for me – which seemed like a nightmare at the time. But really she did me a favour.'

Rosay's eyes scanned the room, but they didn't settle on Amy this time. Had she been looking for Lauren? Did she know it wasn't Amy who had told the world about Scott White after all?

'Though I'm not going to thank her. And the reason for that is that she has stirred up so much trouble among my friends – by posing as a friend – that I've decided I'm not scared of her any more. And anyway she shot herself in the foot when she announced my relationship with Scott. She went one step too far. She was out to get Danny Harris, even if it meant trampling everyone in her path. And she wasn't even after Danny, not really. She wanted to get at his ex. At Claudette. At any cost.' She stopped and added sweetly. 'Isn't that right, Trina?'

This time everyone stared at Trina, who turned and frowned. 'What are you looking at? She's talking rubbish.'

Rosay smiled. 'Wow, Trina. I can see why you like making announcements like this. Makes you feel . . . kind of like you control everyone, doesn't it? And you think you do, don't you? You got all that gossip from Lauren, and some from Kylie and me, and you spread it around – you made it look like Claudette was causing trouble, when for once in her life she wasn't. You wrote to the online gossip sites, didn't you? You worked to make it sound as damaging as possible, for all of us.'

Amy listened in horror. Had Trina written about her online? It was possible. She would have heard a lot of the gossip from Rosay, from Kylie, from Lauren – and even from herself. She remembered Lauren had said she was texting Trina at half-time, during the match when Damien missed his penalty. She'd obviously told Steve about her suspicions to do with Amy and Danny Harris, and that was bad enough. But she'd probably told Trina too – and that's how it had got into the papers.

Then there were the hate texts Amy had received, which she now knew were from Courtney to Lauren. But Trina had told her they were from Claudette. It pointed the finger at Lauren – and at Claudette – and it had played right into Trina's hands. She probably couldn't believe her luck when Amy showed her those.

Amy remembered what Rosay said about Trina holding grudges forever. She must have decided to keep getting at Claudette in any way she could – no matter who else suffered in the process. Amy, for one.

And Rosay. Amy's friend.

And Danny Harris, who seemed to be caught up in this, but who Amy was pretty sure only wanted his ex-wife back.

'You know, though, I don't want this kind of power,' Rosay continued. 'People are saying my career is already taking a nosedive, now that everyone knows I'm going out with Scott White, Britain's most-hated footballer. But guess what?' She paused. 'It doesn't matter what everyone else thinks. It only matters what *I* think. Too many people care way too much about their image – they're running scared of bad publicity and they'd rather hurt themselves, and maybe even damage others, than get it.'

Amy wondered whether Rosay was thinking of her mother, and the terrible time she'd had recovering from her plastic surgery. Then she realized that what Rosay was saying could apply to her too. It was ridiculous how much importance Amy had placed on all the negative publicity she'd had. She'd let it affect her friendships – and her relationship with Damien – even after she'd decided that she didn't care what the press said any more.

'I don't want to be like that,' Rosay continued. 'So I'll keep doing what I love – seeing Scott, singing – whether the world likes it or not.'

There was a long pause. Amy wondered whether to clap – it seemed appropriate – but the rest of the guests just stared at Rosay in stunned silence.

Then Trina started yelling. 'Hear that lack of support, Rosay? The world hates you! And you're a liar! Don't listen to her, anyone! Anyway, Danny knows it's not true! Me and Danny are together, everyone! He couldn't be here tonight, but I know he'd be standing next to me if he could –'

'No, I wouldn't,' a low voice said on stage, and a curtain behind Rosay pulled back to reveal Danny Harris and another footballer dressed up as footmen in tuxedoes, each holding one side of a sedan chair where Kylie was sitting with Poshie on her lap, being lifted along as a petite woman in a hot-pink taffeta dress scattered petals in their path. Then Amy realized the petite woman was Paige Young herself. Maybe they'd all been backstage rehearsing for their big moment, carrying Kylie into the reception like a storybook princess. Amy noticed Johann standing in the wings with a huge smile on his face, admiring Kylie.

'Danny, you told me you couldn't come!' Trina screeched.

'No,' Danny replied gruffly. 'I told you I couldn't come with *you*.'

Trina paused for a second, speechless. Then her voice wavered as she said, 'Rosay Sands, you've just brought yourself a whole heap of trouble!' She hurried out of the room, her head lowered as all eyes turned to her.

Rosay waited a few seconds before she spoke into the microphone again. 'OK, sorry, I've talked far too much. It looks like Kylie's ready, anyway. Kylie?'

The boys lowered the chair and Kylie stepped down, holding a yelping Poshie. She'd changed out of her ballgown-style wedding dress and into a clingy Vera Wang number.

'OK then,' Rosay finished. 'Never mind what you just heard – it's time for the proper big announcement of the night. Kylie and Johann Haag, over to you.'

A murmur went through the guests as Kylie said breathlessly, 'Ladies and gentlemen, thank you for coming to my wedding in Spain. Sorry it was such late notice, but I really wanted Poshie to be the star, you see. Things are going to be hard enough for him soon.'

She tickled Poshie behind the ears and he started to squirm in her arms as if he knew he was being talked about.

'And anyway, we'll probably renew our vows in Wales next year, so you'll all be welcome to another big party . . . with a new star! Or, OK, with *two* stars.' She widened her eyes at her pug. 'Sorry, Poshie. I didn't plan this, you know.'

She put the dog on the ground and he yapped contentedly.

Amy stared. Kylie's dress was *really* figure-hugging – much more than anything Amy had seen her wear this summer. And now that Kylie wasn't holding Poshie, you could clearly see a neat, tiny bump where her super-flat stomach used to be.

'Oh, I nearly forgot the important part! I've been a bit dippy lately, you know,' Kylie said. 'I know it's unlike me to be like that, but I have a good reason. As you can see, I'm pregnant!'

Before anyone could react, there was a scuffle in the background and the sound of female voices shouting. Everyone including Amy turned towards the doorway, just in time to see Lauren and Courtney yelling at Steve, Courtney being held by a security guard who was just about managing to stop her hitting Steve with her sequinned clutch bag.

'You'll regret this!' Courtney was shouting.

'Courtney, don't worry, we'll get him!' Lauren was telling her. 'Me and you both!'

Behind them all was a girl in a black wet-look mini-dress looking shifty and guilty. It was pretty clear that Steve had been caught with her.

The press surrounded Steve as he broke away from the security guard, hurling loud threats. Within seconds, he was restrained by two others, and Courtney was saying loudly to a reporter, 'Tell the world he's abusive! Make sure he never gets on the England squad again! I can tell you a few stories . . .'

Amy really hoped both Lauren and Courtney had broken up with Steve for good this time.

As the security guards got to work and the voices faded

into the distance, Kylie swung her ringlets over one shoulder and remarked, 'My announcements never go very smoothly, do they? Never mind. Just party, everyone! Me and Johann are married now!'

26

The speeches after that had been far less eventful, though possibly equally cringeworthy, and a painful-sounding karaoke session followed. Amy had her suspicions confirmed that nine out of ten footballers absolutely couldn't sing, especially when a group of them attempted the England team song. Though most of the ballers singing played for the Netherlands and maybe they were butchering the song deliberately.

Her phone rang in the middle of a particularly terrible encore and she answered gratefully, even though she half-registered that the call was from her publicist. Well, maybe she could trust him after all, now she was fairly sure it had been Trina, not Claudette, who had called the paps on the day of the *Gabriella* shoot. Rosay must have taken a while to realize Trina was blabbing everything she told her.

'Amy! At last!' her publicist chirped happily. 'I have a fabulous proposal for you! It's a soap drama set on a beach resort, and they want you to play the lifeguard! Will you do it? What do you think?'

'I don't know. I think I need a break. Why don't they consider asking my co-star Asha?' Amy suggested, smiling.

She meant it too. She gave Spencer the details and talked up Asha's skills for a bit.

After that, she wandered around, chatting to guests here and there. Her eyes searched for Damien, but there was no sign of him – or Paige – in the banqueting hall, and she tried not to think about that. Instead, she found Rosay and had a long chat with her, which included loads of apologies, several hugs and an attempt to dance together to Johann Haag's crooning rendition of 'Sweet Caroline' by Neil Diamond, in which he replaced the name 'Caroline' with 'Kylie' and Rosay grumbled that the lyrics didn't even scan.

When Rosay said that there was a distinct lack of men at the party, Amy wondered aloud where Scott was – until she remembered that he probably wasn't invited because he was still the most-hated footballer in Britain.

'He's in Marbella tonight – he travelled down with me – but I couldn't persuade him to come here,' Rosay said. 'I rehearsed my speech in front of him and everything, and he thought it was great, but he said it didn't change the fact that no one would want him here, especially since bloody Trina managed to get him in the papers, and the hate campaign started up all over again. I can't believe I thought Trina was trustworthy!' She sighed. 'Anyway, yeah, Scott refused to be here. Even though Kylie did actually invite him – she's pretty good at giving people second chances, you know.'

'Yeah,' said Amy, slightly distracted as an eager photographer bounded in front of her and snapped a picture of her with Rosay.

'Great, Amy! Can you get a bit closer together, though? It's for *Just Gossip*.'

Amy sighed, though she didn't really mind. She knew her mother would love to see a picture of her with an international pop star, even if Rosay's career was supposedly in trouble.

She put her arm round Rosay and smiled, but the photographer frowned.

'I meant you and Damien. I've heard all the rumours that you're not together any more and it would be great to get the scoop that all is well with "Amien". Our readers love you two – you're like the couple of the year.' He added quickly. 'Apart from Kylie and Johann, of course.'

'And me and Scott?' Rosay smirked.

'Well, not exactly . . . Er, yes, of course! So Amy if you could just . . .'

But Amy wasn't listening any more, and neither was Rosay. They'd turned round to see Damien behind them. With Scott White.

'Hi, Ames,' Damien said with a nervous smile.

'Damien!' Amy tried to control her heart, which was suddenly hammering.

Rosay squealed and threw her arms around Scott, pulling him aside and away from where Amy and Damien were staring at each other.

'You're here,' Amy said, wishing she could sound less pathetic.

'Yeah,' said Damien 'Only till ten o'clock, though.'

'But you can't still have a curfew! The World Cup's over! And sorry you didn't win, by the way, but you were amazing!

That penalty was fantastic. And all the rest of your playing too.'

He smiled again. 'Thanks, Ames. Yeah, no, it's not a curfew exactly, but Joe Vulkan's organized this special night out. Only Netherlands players and Boroughs players were invited to this wedding, you know.'

'Oh, right.'

'Yeah, and it's just that Joe Vulkan expects us all to be there. It's a team thing. Look, sorry I didn't see you sooner, but I was late so I was right at the back, and then I heard Rosay's speech and I decided to go and call Scott. I thought I'd get him to come here, you know, for Rosay. I had to persuade Paige to give me his number first, though.'

'Oh. Oh, yeah,' Amy stuttered. She was amazed that Damien would do that for Scott and Rosay, when she knew Damien didn't particularly like either of them. Not to mention the fact that Paige would hand over Scott's number. She was the last of Scott's exes before Rosay, and she was notoriously jealous.

It all reminded Amy that Paige and Damien were really close friends.

'Yeah, she's over him,' Damien explained. 'Paige is over a lot of her problems. More or less. But you know, I heard what Rosay said, and so did Paige. Plus I think Scott's perfect for Rosay. They're right for each other.' His smile was a bit wicked, and Amy was sure he didn't mean that in a good way.

'You're still not close enough!' The photographer waved his hand at the space between Amy and Damien.

'Get *them* instead,' Amy said, nodding towards Scott and Rosay, who were now in the middle of a passionate kiss.

Rosay was obviously keen to prove she didn't care about what the press said. Scott didn't seem to mind going along with it.

'But they're not football's golden couple,' the photographer grumbled. 'They don't shift papers like you two.'

Amy smiled at him. 'Don't people like you change things like that, depending on the angle you take with your pictures?'

Then, without a second glance at the photographer, she said to Damien, 'Come on. I've had enough of cameras.'

Amy wound her way through the castle with Damien following. They stopped on a quiet floodlit turret, overlooking a swathe of darkness and the distant twinkling of lights near the seafront.

She looked at Damien for a long moment, but he glanced shiftily around, his Adam's apple bobbing like he was beyond nervous.

Why was he acting like that? And so distant too. Was this it – was it really over between them? She wished she could just ask him.

Finally he looked at her. 'Amy . . .'

'No wait. Me first.' Amy took a deep breath. 'I want to ask you something, OK?'

Damien nodded.

'OK.' Then she wasn't exactly sure how to ask him. She decided to be direct. 'So first . . . are you seeing Paige Young? I mean, you know . . .' She gave up. 'Well, you know.'

Damien shook his head. 'No! Course not, Ames. I told you. We –'

Amy held up her hand for him to stop. 'It's OK, you don't have to explain. I just wanted to check, because people keep telling me you are. So, also . . .' This was harder. Amy thought she'd known the answer to the first question, despite the doubts everyone seemed determined to put in her mind.

But this . . . She really wasn't sure of this at all.

'I was going to ask you . . .' She lost her nerve slightly. 'You know, I've sort of been tired of the way we keep falling out and . . . you know . . . you not seeing me, and you not ringing me . . .'

'You asked me not to ring you!'

'I know. But still, you didn't. And I know there's something you want to say to me.' She blinked a lot, then she said it. 'So you can tell me now. Is it . . . is it over between us?'

Damien stepped forward and put his arms round her. He said quietly, 'I hope not.'

Amy was desperate to kiss him then, but she forced herself to pull back from the amazing feel of his arms. 'What were you going to say before, then? If you weren't going to finish with me?'

'I was going to say I had a plan,' he said. 'You know, to keep us together. The distance thing isn't working – it's obvious. So I thought of asking for a transfer up north. I could talk to my agent about it! It might have to be a lower division team, but . . .'

'Damien, do you want a transfer?'

'No, not really, but . . .'

'Well then, don't ask for one. Please. Anyway, I don't know if . . .'

'What?'

'I don't know if that would be the answer. Seeing you more, I mean.'

He stared at her. 'OK,' he said slowly. 'So what exactly are *you* saying?' He took a step away from her and stared at the ground.

'I'm saying . . . we definitely have a problem. As you know. Because I'm not sure . . . I'm not sure if I can do it.'

'Right,' he said quietly, turning away from her. 'I get it. I know you nearly finished with me before, that day in San Sebastian. I just hoped . . .'

'No, wait!' Amy's voice rose with frustration. 'Let me explain. You were right before, with what you said – this isn't me. Being in the spotlight, being famous for being your girlfriend. I don't want to worry about everything I say to everyone all the time, and how it gets reported and distorted. I don't want to be affected by what it says in the papers. It was horrible when it felt like the world hated me.' Amy paused. 'But I'm not sure it's any better now – now that they're saying I'm some kind of hero. You know, I'm just me.'

'I know.' Damien turned back and looked at her. 'I know exactly what you mean.'

Amy frowned. 'Do you?'

'Yeah. Course. It's exactly the same for me. I just want to play football. But every time I get on the pitch, I know that if I score a winning goal, or even just play enough good balls, it will mean praise all over. If I get it wrong, they won't let me forget it.'

'They won't let *me* forget it,' Amy corrected him.

She was half-joking, but he didn't smile, 'Yeah. OK. And that's really unfair. No wonder you've had enough.' He ran a hand through his short hair. 'I'm gutted. I really didn't want this to happen. I didn't want us to break up. You've no idea, Ames.'

She bit her lip and stared at the lights in the distance. 'I don't want us to break up either!'

He gave her a confused look. 'But it's like you said. Like we both said. You're right. That stuff's all part of my life. But you . . . You don't have to do this, Amy. Not, you know . . . Not if you're not with me.'

'But I want to be with you! You're the one who's behaving as if it's not what *you* want!'

'Amy. I want *you*.' He moved forwards, put his hands on her shoulders and looked deep into her eyes. He sighed. 'You know what? Lately, when I'm with you, I feel like I'm just stepping out on to the pitch and anything could happen.' He touched the ends of her hair, lowering his eyes. 'It's terrifying. But you know how I get through it when I'm playing football?'

Amy shook her head.

'I don't think about winning or losing. I don't worry about the outcome, or what my manager or the press will think of what I'm doing. I just play. Know what I mean?'

'Yeah,' she said. She stepped into his arms. 'Yeah, I get it.' She pressed her body into his and her mouth against his mouth.

He returned her kiss and they melted into each other, kissing for so long that, eventually, Amy realized Damien must be late for Joe Vulkan. She pulled away, ready to say goodnight, no longer worrying about what it meant for them, because right now things were fantastic, and that was what mattered.

'You have to go,' she told him. 'The manager of England is waiting for you, remember?'

But he smiled, shrugged lightly and drew her closer.

And Amy knew for sure that they'd live to play another day.

Read an extract from the first book
in this wildly addictive new series

WAGS' World
Playing the Game

By
Anonymous

1

For Amy Thornton, the party was almost perfect.

Chandeliers hung over luxurious furnishings in a room that was probably big enough to contain an entire football pitch. A staff of black-clad waitresses, all around Amy's age, smiled professionally as they swept by, offering silver trays of fancy nibbles. Huddles of glamorous, barely dressed girls laughed together and behaved every inch like they felt right at home in this glitzy mansion.

Amy was holding an elaborate-looking canapé on a stick and a fluted glass of champagne cocktail she'd been told was called a Meringue Royale.

It was all wonderful. But there was something missing.

Not something. Someone.

Damien.

Damien Taylor, rising star, who had made the move from Stanleydale United to the Royal Boroughs for a sum of money that got all the tabloids in a frenzy. Boy wonder, tipped for greatness, his name already pencilled in football's hall of fame.

Or rather: Damien Taylor, Amy's first and only boyfriend, the boy-literally-next-door from their West Yorkshire hometown. The boy who, two years ago, had stammeringly asked her out and then kissed her at the bowling alley. And they'd been totally, amazingly in love ever since. So much so that she'd saved up money from her weekend and holiday job and come all the way to London so they could spend the rest of summer side by side.

Except that he wasn't here.

Instead of Damien, she had Rosay ('*Like the wine*') standing next to her. Her new friend was scanning the room and explaining in gossipy detail exactly what was wrong with every victim her eyes landed on. Amy made polite noises in response. She'd only been in London a few hours and she wouldn't have felt right commenting on the dress sense and dating history of total strangers.

She didn't mean to, but she found herself tuning Rosay out and beginning a private game of 'spot the celebrity' instead, trying not to stare too much. It felt like some kind of dream, being surrounded by all these famous faces.

She gave herself three points for the actress and the girl-band member she spotted, and two each for the models, although she wasn't completely sure about those – most of the women here looked like models anyway. She only awarded herself one point for every footballer she recognized. It was a footballer's party, after all.

She'd already seen the party's host a couple of times, each time with his arm around a different woman, neither of whom were his girlfriend. But Damien wasn't the only absent team member, which could explain things. A few of them must have been asked to stay behind after the match.

Her sleb-spotting score was well into double figures when she heard Rosay say, 'Of course, everyone knows that there's no such thing as a faithful footballer, especially in the Premier League.'

Amy snapped out of her trance. 'I'm sure that isn't true.'

'It's very true. Not one, not ever. They're all the same.' Rosay's laugh was hollow. 'Sooner or later, they all cheat.'

Amy was sure that Rosay had been hurt in the past – she seemed to have an axe to grind, and she'd been chopping away all afternoon.

Rosay went on about temptation, boys being boys and footballers being anyone's. 'Seriously, Amy, you're lucky I'm here to warn you. Most of us find out the hard way.'

Amy brushed that comment aside. Damien wasn't that kind of guy. Her hand was immediately drawn to the delicate Tiffany necklace he'd given her when he moved to London. At the time, she'd joked that he should have bought something more practical instead. She could do with a new suitcase, for a start. But he'd said no; he wanted to get her something beautiful and long-lasting. But it wasn't the expensive heart-shaped pendant that made her sure of Damien; it was everything it stood for. Damien loved her. Damien was nothing like whoever had broken Rosay's heart.

Amy fiddled with the diamond cluster on the pendant. 'Look, I'm sorry. I've had a tiring day. I think I'll go back to the house,' she told Rosay, hoping it didn't sound too rude. After all, she'd been really lovely, going out of her way to help Amy adjust to this strange environment.

But she really should get back. Damien couldn't even contact her here. Rosay had insisted Amy leave her mobile behind because it would ruin the line of the tiny Miu Miu clutch bag she'd lent her. Even lip gloss and a key were testing its limits.

Anyway, surely after whatever had kept him, Damien would rush back to the house to see her. He was probably there right now, wondering where she was. He certainly wouldn't expect her to be all glammed up at some party he hadn't even mentioned to her.

But just then a rumble of deep voices filled the enormous space. Amy heard loud laughter accompanied by a chorus of 'One–nil!', 'Nice one!', 'Trounced 'em!' and various other celebratory calls as a group of men piled into the party.

It was the rest of the Royal Boroughs boys. They sounded a lot like Stanleydale's local team, but there was no doubt they looked different. Cleaner and smarter, for a start. And surrounded by girls who sparkled more brightly than the diamanté studs on Rosay's belt.

'You can't leave now,' Rosay declared. 'The rest of the boys have arrived!'

That's when, through the throng, Amy caught the words, 'Way-hey, the new boy's pulled at last! Fit bird, Taylor!' They were coming from a guy Amy thought she recognized as the Boroughs goalie, who had a leery smirk on his face. She followed his gaze.

And there he was at last. Damien – *her* Damien.

He was standing with a familiar-looking girl in a skimpy gold dress, and she was laughing as if he'd said something hilarious, and holding on to his arm.

Rosay gave Amy a worried look.

The gold-clad girl was none other than the chronic boyfriend-stealer Rosay had been warning her about all day.

Will Amy's indulgent shopping sprees come back to haunt her?
And what will happen when she falls into a trap of blackmail and scandal?

Find out in the second book in this wildly addictive new series . . .

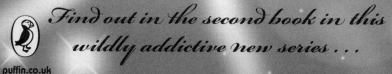

It all started with a Scarecrow.

Puffin is seventy years old.

Sounds ancient, doesn't it? But Puffin has never been
so lively. We're always on the lookout for the next big
idea, which is how it began all those years ago.

Penguin Books was a big idea from the mind of
a man called Allen Lane, who in 1935 invented
the quality paperback and changed the world.
**And from great Penguins, great Puffins grew,
changing the face of children's books forever.**

The first four Puffin Picture Books were hatched in 1940 and the
first Puffin story book featured a man with broomstick arms called
Worzel Gummidge. In 1967 Kaye Webb, Puffin Editor, started the
Puffin Club, promising to **'make children into readers'**.
She kept that promise and over 200,000 children became
devoted Puffineers through their quarterly instalments of
Puffin Post, which is now back for a new generation.

Many years from now, we hope you'll look back and
remember Puffin with a smile. **No matter what your age
or what you're into, there's a Puffin for everyone.**
The possibilities are endless, but one thing is for sure:
whether it's a picture book or a paperback, a sticker book
or a hardback, **if it's got that little Puffin
on it – it's bound to be good.**